GILBERT-AUGUSTIN THIERRY

REINCARNATION
AND
REDEMPTION

TRANSLATED AND WITH AN INTRODUCTION BY
BRIAN STABLEFORD

I0689490

REINCARNATION
AND
REDEMPTION

GILBERT-AUGUSTIN THIERRY (1843-1915), the son of the writer Amédée Thierry and the nephew of the historian Augustin Thierry, was a novelist, poet and journalist, who published extensively in the *Revue des Deux-Mondes*. In 1875 he debuted with the intensively-researched historical novel *L'Aventure d'une âme en peine*, followed in 1882 by *Le Capitaine Sans-Façon 1813: épisodes de la contre-révolution*. His subsequent works, which include *Marfa* (1887), *La tresse blonde* (1888), *La Savelli* (1890), *Le masque* (1894) and *Le stigmate* (1898), often dealt with the occult and the supernatural.

BRIAN STABLEFORD'S scholarly work includes *New Atlantis: A Narrative History of Scientific Romance* (Wildside Press, 2016), *The Plurality of Imaginary Worlds: The Evolution of French roman scientifique* (Black Coat Press, 2017) and *Tales of Enchantment and Disenchantment: A History of Faerie* (Black Coat Press, 2019). In support of the latter projects he has translated more than a hundred volumes of *roman scientifique* and more than twenty volumes of *contes de fées* into English. He has edited *Decadence and Symbolism: A Showcase Anthology* (Snuggly Books, 2018), and is busy translating more Symbolist and Decadent fiction.

His recent fiction, in the genre of metaphysical fantasy, includes a trilogy of novels set in West Wales, consisting of *Spirits of the Vasty Deep* (2018), *The Insubstantial Pageant* (2018) and *The Truths of Darkness* (2019), published by Snuggly Books, and a trilogy set in Paris and the south of France, consisting of *The Painter of Spirits*, *The Quiet Dead* and *Living with the Dead*, all published by Black Coat Press in 2019.

CONTENTS

Introduction / 7

Larmor's Redemption / 15
Rediviva / 55
The Beloved / 89

INTRODUCTION

The first two novelettes contained in this volume were originally published in *La Nouvelle Revue*, "La Rédemption de Larmor," here translated as "Larmor's Redemption" in the 1 April 1882 issue and "Rediviva" in the 1 November 1883 issue. They were advertised as the first two items in a series entitled "Histoires de Mort et de Vivants, récits étranges" [Accounts of the Dead and the Living: Strange Stories], but no further items appeared in *La Nouvelle Revue*. The author signed them with the by-line Gilbert-Augustin Thierry, which was his real name, although many reference books render it as Gilbert Augustin-Thierry, an alternative signature that he also sometimes employed, and which he attached to the novella completing the present collection, "La Bien-Aimée" (tr. as "The Beloved") when it appeared in the *Revue des Deux Mondes* in December 1891.

Gilbert-Augustin Thierry (1843-1915) was given his second forename after his uncle, the noted historian Augustin Thierry (1795-1856), who was more scrupulous in his consultation of documentary evidence than many historians of the era but routinely adopted a colorful narrativized style of reportage that affiliated him strongly to the French Romantic Movement. It was Augustin Thierry's enduring fame that encouraged his nephew to transplant the hyphen in his signature in his later works. Gilbert's father, Amédée Thierry (1797-1873), who was also significantly associated with the Romantic Movement, was a historian too, although he obtained his principal reputation as a journalist—a profession that he was initially obliged to adopt because he was dismissed from the chair of history at Besançon for being too liberal in his opinions during the repressive reign of Charles X. That guaranteed him considerable favor after the July Revolution of 1830, when he was appointed prefect of the Haut-Saône, and he held various other administrative posts before and after the 1848 Revolution before becoming a Senator in 1860. In the meantime, he was a regular contributor to the *Revue des Deux Mondes*, which began as a Radical Romantic publication but, like him, shifted to the right in response to changes in the political climate after Louis-Napoléon's 1851 *coup-d'état*.

Gilbert followed in his father's footsteps, publishing extensively in the *Revue des Deux Mondes* and enjoying a successful career in journalism, but he was also heavily influenced by his uncle; he became an assiduous researcher and employer of documentary sources, and he followed S. Henry Berthoud's example in labeling many of his works of fiction "historical studies" in order to emphasize their scholarly underpinnings. His work might, however, also be held to illustrate that an assiduous interest in exceedingly unreliable documentary sources can easily tempt a historian, however scrupulous he might be, to eccentric conclusions. It is also arguable that his intellectual scrupulousness soon became questionable; he became very interested in and heavily involved with the French Occult Revival—which began as an offshoot of the Romantic Movement in the movement's decadent phase—and much of his fiction was written under that influence, including his first novel, the intensively-researched *L'Aventure d'une âme en peine* [The Adventure of a Soul in Pain] (1875).

As a result of his occult research, the supernatural became much more explicit in Thierry's later works, beginning with the two novelettes in the present volume and the first of a complementary series of novellas in the *Revue des Deux Mondes*, "Le Palimpseste" (March 1887 in the periodical; reprinted in book form in the same year as *Marfa, ou Le Palimpseste*; tr. as *The*

Palimpsest). It is not obvious why the series switched periodicals, but the *Revue des Deux Mondes* might simply have been more hospitable to longer stories. At any rate, all the remaining stories that can be seen in retrospect as components of the series appeared in the *Revue des Deux Mondes*: *La Blonde Tresse* [The Blonde Tress] (July 1888; in book form 1889), *Le Masque* [The Mask] (January-February 1894; in book form 1894), *Le Stigmate* [Stigma] (July-August 1897; in book form 1898) and "La Fresque de Pompei" [The Pompeian Fresco] (March 1912). Translations of those four novellas, in two pairs, will feature in supplements to the present volume.

Like the work of many of the writers closely associated with the Occult Revival, Gilbert-Augustin Thierry's fiction has attracted little attention from lovers of fantastic fiction, partly because of its propagandistic element, although the relative rarity of the book versions of the longer stories helped to maintain them in obscurity. His work might also have seemed a trifle dated after the turn of the century, not so much because of its recherché nature as because of its sometimes-feverish melodramatic Romantic affiliation. The association in question contrived a peculiar hybridization similar to that exhibited in his uncle's work and carried forward by other Romantic narrative historians like Jules Michelet and Edgar Quinet, and such conspicuously Romantic writers of historical fiction as S. Henry Berthoud and Victor Hugo. The chimerical compounds resulting from that twofold interest were in decline even in the latter part of the nineteenth century, and became rarer in the twentieth, even though a substantial subgenre of historical fiction retained very evident Romantic aspirations, and still retains them stubbornly to the present day.

The particular emphasis of Thierry's occult fiction differs from the literary work of such contemporary affiliates of the Occult Revival as Joséphin Peladan, Jules Bois, Victor-Émile Michelet and Jane de La Vaudère because of its intense preoccupation with a particular notion of reincarnation. Many French occultists accepted the notion that souls carry forward burdens of sin from previous incarnations, which hinder the continuing moral progress of the entity in question unless the heritage in question can be expiated to some degree. In that world-view, the essential purpose of reiterated existence is a slow and difficult progress toward a hypothetical moral perfection, which provides a context for present conduct.

Such notions often feature in the background of occult fictions, usually as discoveries to be made in the course of a story, which supposedly explain odd circumstances, in the same way that people still occasionally search for "explanations" for their present distress in terms of experiences in their "past lives," sometimes seeking assisted psychological regression in order to discover those explanatory factors. Thierry, however, invariably goes further than that, focusing not on the quest for discovery but on the behavioral consequences of the awareness—or, conversely, on the refusal to accept the implications of the revelation by seeking the necessary redemption of the inherited burden. That is the central theme of the three stories here, which carefully contrast the two alternatives, thus putting in place "boundary markers" that bracketed the author's future explorations of the theme. The three stories also demonstrate the progressive evolution of the notion within Thierry's work; the second story lays down groundwork for the third, which is more elaborate and more sophisticated in terms of both its occult hypotheses and its narrative strategy.

Because Thierry's work takes the thesis of reincarnation for granted rather than employing it as a narrative revelation, his supernatural stories seem to be further along the spectrum of suspended disbelief than most fiction dealing with the theme, plunging readers directly into an imaginative environment that writers of fiction often prefer to approach more stealthily, easing the reader's acceptance of the supernatural hypothesis for the purposes of the narrative. The latter strategy is much more conducive to the writing of horror stories, in which the gradual revelation facilitates the building of dramatic tension. The narrative dynamics of Thierry's fiction are much more idiosyncratic, and although his stories certainly contain an element of horror, its cultivation is not the principal purpose of the stories, which are much more concerned with metaphysical fascination. They are, however, interesting examples of an intriguing subspecies of supernatural fiction, and they certainly have no lack of narrative verve and flamboyance.

The three translations were made from the copies of the relevant issues of *La Nouvelle Revue* and the *Revue des Deux Mondes* reproduced on the Bibliothèque Nationale's gallica website. Thierry's punctuation tends to be idiosyncratic, particularly with reference to the employment of entire lines of dots to indicate gaps in source manuscripts from which he is allegedly copying. I have modified his usages slightly, but have tried to preserve the eccentric spirit of the originals.

—Brian Stableford.

REINCARNATION
AND
REDEMPTION

LARMOR'S REDEMPTION

. . . .

So I picked up the manuscript that my savant friend, poor Victor Longchamp, had bequeathed me—a very long manuscript, believe me, and entirely written in the hand of a deceased archeologist. At first sight it seemed to be incomplete and full of lacunae: here and there, several blank sheets interrupted the text; in many places, lines of dots served as a transition or replaced a chapter. The author had not had time to finish his work.

At the head of the first page there was a sentence traced in capital letters, a bizarre text, an epigraph of mysterious meaning:

BY VIRTUE OF THREE THINGS A MAN
FALLS BACK INTO THE NECESSITY OF
ABRED: THE ABSENCE OF EFFORT TOWARD
KNOWLEDGE, THE MISUNDERSTANDING
OF GOOD AND THE PRACTICE OF EVIL.

At that point, my savant friend had put an explanatory gloss in the margin:

"ABRED, *vulgo* the Inferno down below; rather, in my opinion, the Inferno down here. Thus, three things bring one back to the Inferno of life: ignorance, scorn of the good, and the practice of evil."

Very intrigued by such a logogriph, I struggled for a few minutes trying to comprehend the incomprehensible enigma. But, having been unable to succeed, I turned the page and I read:

I

It was in the month of April 1875 that the first volume of my *Essay on the Bardic Triads of Iolo Morganwg*[1] appeared from the academic publisher Didier et Cie.

To tell the truth, that book, whose sole defect is an overly modest title, could have been called *The History of Human Religion*.

A convinced adversary of Biblical traditions, I denied from the outset the divinity of Eloha, the mud-kneader of Eden, and I even mocked that strange God who "takes the air every evening, when the wind rises" on the banks of the river Pison and the river Gihon.[2] "No," I said to him, daring to speak rudely, "I refuse to bow my head before you, who forbade human beings to know, when the very essence of humanity is to learn; you, who have not understood that all good comes from science and that all evil is nothing but ignorance of the god. With your negative law, you might perhaps have formed the brute, but you never created human beings."

After Eloha and his transformation into Jehovah I studied the Christian God. That illogical and unreasonable being, who chastises or recompenses the finite by means of the infinite; who, in his Inferno, does not improve the sin but avenges himself on the sinner—that inventor of the eternity of punishment—was proclaimed by me to be worthy of all human disdain. "Sorry creator," I also said to that one, "who, responsible for social misery, have only found for an excuse the remark that 'The poor will always be among you!'"

I dared even more. Not content with denying the Gods of the Church, I did not hesitate to attack all the deities worshiped at the Institut:

---

1 "Iolo Morganwg" was the "Bardic name" of the Welsh antiquarian Edward Williams (1747-1826), who is now believed to have forged many of the "triads" that he passed off as translations from Medieval Welsh.

2 Pison and Gihon are two of the four rivers said in *Genesis* to flow out of Eden.

the Bel of Chaldea who, floating impassively in the azure of his Oriental sky, pours his radiance indifferently over the good as over the evil;

the Api of Egypt, the incarnate with the big round eyes, who contemplates the fellah without compassion and the Pharaoh without anger;

the Zeus of the Hellenes, that immortal born of Time, not of Eternity, who, by virtue of his passions, made himself more miserably human than humans;

and Allah, that other Semite, as infantile as all Semites, that fanatic of himself, who demands of humans not virtue, but faith.

Finally, the doctrine of Nirvana, the Buddhist annihilation, in spite of his followers, more numerous every day in Europe, extracted unworthy protestations from me.

Only one God appeared to me to be truly divine: the one who had been worshiped by the noblest of the Aryans, the Gallo-Cymri, our forefathers. With what admiration I exposed the religious philosophy of the druidic triads: the perpetuity of life through death; the necessary reincarnation of all beings until the final amelioration; the successive transformism of the soul, the complement of the transformism of the body, one by the selection of the Beautiful, the other by the selection of the Good; the redemption of a bad life by an unhappy life; poverty the expiation of wealth, tears of laughter and hunger of greed—in brief, the perpetual ascension of every animate being from world to world, though space, until the total annihilation in the One who is Light, Justice and Truth.

"I have crossed your summits," I cried, in a moment of enthusiasm, "O gigantic dolmens of Carnac and Gawr'innis, sepulchral mountains, glorious tombs in which the great chiefs with the necklaces of jade, the powerful manipulators of flint axes, slept inviolate for such a long time! And seeing you standing so high above the plain, I understood the meaning of your structure—emblems of Death dominating Life . . .

"But down there, sown in the heathland like the crop in the fields, I perceived the menhirs springing from the earth to launch themselves toward space, and I understood again, and I saluted in them Life, daughter of Death . . .

"Then, oh, then, a cry of admiration rose toward You, who revealed all these things to our forefathers; and I worshiped you on my knees; on my knees I wanted to love you, for you alone are my God, you who, by expiation, constrain human beings to become gods, O merciful justice, O implacable benevolence."

In any other land than our land of France, the appearance of such a book would have excited public curiosity violently. In Germany, that philosophical battlefield, applause or protests would have risen up from every university; Bel, Api, Zeus or Jehovah would have had their partisans or their detractors. Alas, very different was the welcome given by our population of *Welches*[1] to the Essay on the Bardic Triads. What an icy silence and what indifference! Messieurs of the *Figaro* remained mute; even the messieurs of *Le Temps* maintained a strict silence. Only infimal technical journals devoted a few lines to my work, in order to pour criticism upon it, not to say outrage. In the *Année historique*, a colleague who prudently maintained his anonymity, declared that my "nonsense" did not merit the honor of an analysis, but he joked ponderously about the "poetics of my style" and the "flowers of my rhetoric." Two Catholic newspapers treated me as a "firebrand of Hell" and, in the deplorable style that is fashionable today among the French clergy, demanded that my book should immediately be placed on the Index . . .

And that was all!

The indifference of the public and the attacks of the malevolent produced their fruits. The proprietor of the firm of Didier

---

1 The German word *Velches* or *Welches* [foreigners] was once frequently applied with scathing contempt to the French and Italians in particular.

et Cie announced to me in a heartbroken tone that the edition of the *Essay on the Bardic Triads* was encumbering the cellars of his bookshop almost in its entirety; he had not even sold twenty copies! Furthermore, that timorous man declared to me that I must renounce the publication of my second volume. O dolor! Such, then, was the recompense accorded in my homeland to so much labor! And I fled; I ran away from Paris. On the first of August I was in Carnac.

The old stones of the old menhirs, friends so long cultivated by me, I was avid to see you again; I wanted to tell you about my sadness and receive your consolations, you who had informed me in your great silent language. Yes, I was desperate! And yet, the Persian poet says: "Let the bite of the envious be milder to your flesh than the kiss of the beloved woman." A sentence that is assuredly admirable, albeit formulated by an author who is perhaps apocryphal.

II

. . . .

"Bonjour, Madame Lautrem!"

The mistress of the Hôtel des Voyageurs quit the fireplace with the vast mantle, where roasting meat was crackling, and came to meet the person who was calling to her.

"Why, it's you, Monsieur Longchamp! You've come back to us!"

"And for a long time, I hope, my good Madame Lautrem. Can you give me a room, then . . . the best of your rooms, if you please?"

The good Madame Lautrem put her hands together

"Jesus and Mary! A room? A room for you, all to yourself?"

"Of course."

"Oh, Holy Virgin! Typical of those men who occupy themselves with antiquities: always with the dead, never with the living. But look, my dear Monsieur, look out there!"

And the lady's finger extended in the direction of the square of the church.

The square was, in fact, overflowing with people, and a confused hubbub was rising into the air. A few Venetian masts, stuck in the ground, were allowing their tricolor pennants to undulate; a few fairground booths were exhibiting, with a noisy concert of big drums, two-headed calves, sword-swallowers or *odalisque-torpilles*;[1] and in front of the façade of the Mairie, was a stage hung with superb red calico. A buzzing Breton crowd was coming and going along the village's only street: men from Vannes in black jackets, men from Hennebont in blue jackets; men from Pontivy in white ones. And, just as joyful as the young men, the girls were clad in their finery, those from Auray with heavy bonnets and pigeon-throat aprons, and those from Elven with large saffron-colored headscarves; pretentious pretty girls from the Île d'Arz and tall prudish brunettes from the Île aux Moines; and others who had come from further away, from the region of Quimperlé, where every respectable young woman hides her hair modestly under a nun's head-dress and wears a folded collaret falling all the way to the hips. Everyone was drunk, prodigiously drunk, reeking of cider, hiccupping eau-de-vie—especially the women.

"The Agricultural Show!" I exclaimed, fearfully.

"Yes, the Agricultural Show," said Madame Lautrem, vaingloriously. "The Sub-Prefect is lodging here, in uniform, and the messieurs of the district council have come with him, three general councilors, a député, and the noblemen with their wives. The festival will last a week. The day after tomorrow, the speeches; this evening, dancing to the bagpipes. I don't have a single room

---

1 The wordplay of this phrase is complicated; there was something of a fad in the late nineteenth century for the exhibition in fairgrounds of "electric boys" who could deliver electric shocks by means of static electricity. On the other hand, *torpille* [literally, electric ray or eel] had long been a vulgar term employed with regard to prostitutes, although "*odalisque-torpilles*" might simply be belly-dancers.

free, but I can set up a bed for you in the grain-loft—and that, Monsieur Longchamp, only because it's you . . ."

"The Show!" I repeated again, fearfully. "Keep your bed, Madame Lautrem; I'm leaving, and right away, for Quiberon. I'll go to Saint-Pierre; there are the remains of an alignment of five menhirs there, and, above all, silence. Quickly! A carriage and a horse!"

The hotelier started to smile and shrugged her shoulders. "Oh yes, a carriage and a horse! But you won't find a carriole or a bourriquet in the entire region. The people at the Show have taken everything."

She saw my air of desperation, and doubtless felt sorry for me, because she added: "Tomorrow morning, but very early, Monsieur Gestas is going by sea to Quiberon. Do you know him?"

That name, Gestas, made me start abruptly. Gestas! What a bizarre name!

"Do you know him?"

"I don't know him." Then, gathering my memories: "Gestas? But, in our ancient mysteries, that's the name of the thief crucified to the right of Jesus Christ, the reprobate who was the first to be ransomed from Hell. Gestas! Gestas! What a strange name!"

Madame Lautrem looked at me disdainfully. "If you were a Breton, Monsieur, if you had fought with our lads at the battle of Le Mans,[1] you'd know the name of Monsieur Gestas."

I wasn't listening. The text of a Mystery Play had suddenly returned to mind: "'Gestas,' said the Lord, 'enter into Paradise.' Oh, adorable naivety of ancient authors! Oh, exquisite charm of . . ."

"Monsieur," said Madame Lautrem, a pious and stern woman, "I don't like hearing the good Lord mocked, the Holy Virgin, the saints in paradise and our Mother Church."

---

1 The Bartle of Le Mans (10-12 January 1871) was a disaster for the French resistance to the invading German armies in the Franco-Prussian War. 25,000 French soldiers were killed and 50,000 deserted.

With that, the lady turned her back on me and went toward the fireplace to rejoin her maidservants.

"Madame! My dear lady . . ."

Bah! She was no longer listening, entirely occupied now with the difficult launch of an omelet on to the stove. I took out a visiting card and laid it on the table.

"Ask your Monsieur on my behalf for the favor of climbing into his boat tomorrow."

And I left.

While walking through the crowd, however, I repeated aloud: "Gestas! Gestas!" Like an obsession, the verse of the old Mystery Play harassed my mind: "Gestas," said the Lord, "enter into Paradise."

. . . .

III

. . . .

How desperate the voice of your bells seems, church of old Carnac, when, at the decline of the day, it awakens with its plaint the vast slumber of the torpid heathland!

Dusk was falling. The last glimmers of the sun were dying away in the ocean, setting the waves ablaze and speckling the sands of Quiberon with sparks. Toward the east, darkness was veiling the sky, already pierced by the scintillation of stars, and in the distance, the great fir-plantations of Kerlescant were filed with shadow and terror. The road that ran past the tumulus of Saint-Michel, that sepulchral mountain, was cluttered with joyful people; people were singing and shouting—the last echoes of the day's festival. The bagpipes were making their shrill notes heard, and reed flutes, the monotonous *bombardes*, were responding, even more highly-pitched. Soon, men taking one another by the hand were beginning to dance the *hroal*.

A strange farandole, the Breton hroal! In cadence, everyone balances on the left leg, and then on the right, leaps ponderously on both feet, and recommences the hop and skip. "Blow! Blow! Couëdic! Blow till you burst, old pagan!"

And he blew and blew, the old pagan, like a frank Devil's fiddler, without pausing for breath. Crouched on the ground, to either side of the road, the women watched the dance, motionless and silent.

With voices and gestures, our lads teased them. "Come on, come on, Yvonette, your four lovers are quivering with us! And you, Corentine the prude, are you so scared of M'sieu le Curé?" Wasted gibes; Yvonnette and Corentine don't budge; there's still too much light . . .

And the shadow enveloped us, denser from moment to moment, and the bagpipe and the bombarde whined their three notes with no truce or repose.

Finally, no longer able to stand it, a girl got up, and with a bound, threw herself into the dance. A clamor of joy welcomed her arrival. "Good for you! Good for you!" Then two, ten, twenty women launched themselves likewise; hands interlaced; the *hroal* unwound, snaking and twisting, black against the white dust of the road.

The voice of one dancer rose up, singing a ballad taken up in chorus:

> *In trouble, in work,*
> *In all amusements,*
> *I never forget my love,*
> *She's always on my mind.*

Lying in the heather, at the foot of a dry stone wall—the habitual enclosure of Breton fields—I allowed myself to be lulled by the chant, savoring pleasurably the great forgetfulness of myself.

O indelible vestiges of our primal origin, I said to myself, *one finds you everywhere. Is not the Breton* hroal *the syrtos of the*

Hellenes. Doubtless borrowed from the first Aryans, and by the Aryans themselves . . .

"Darling!" murmured a voice nearby, in English. "My Bella, how I love you!"

"No, Harris," replied another voice. "No, you don't know how to love!"

I raised my eyes. A man and a woman were standing a few paces away. They were amorously enlaced, the man holding the woman by the waist, the woman leaning her head on the man's shoulder. Completely lost in the shadow of the wall, I could see them, but they could not see me.

"Harris O'Riordan," said the woman, in a mocking tone, "how courageous you are this evening! One can tell that *he* isn't here."

And that *he* was pronounced in an indefinable tone in which hatred, anger and scorn vibrated simultaneously.

"*He,*" she continued, "is practicing at this moment one of his habitual sacrileges; he's evoking the dead and blaspheming the Omnipotent. Why haven't you gone with him, Harris?"

The man she had just called Harris O'Riordan replied: "He forbade me to go with him."

And a frisson appeared to agitate his limbs.

The woman laughed heartily. "How you're trembling, my poor friend, and how frightened you are!"

"Yes, I'm afraid," said the man, in a dull voice, gradually becoming animated. "I'm afraid because he's a terrible seer. Look around you, Bella, don't you recognize these places, about which he talks incessantly? This land where, he affirms, an O'Riordan, my grandfather, once lived. There's Mont Saint-Michel, the enormous tomb where the unknown dead, whom he knows, have been sleeping for so many centuries. Further away, there are the stones of bizarre form, and the heathland that souls take pleasure in haunting, where the living can converse with the dead. Look again: those dunes that are plunging into the ocean; isn't that Quiberon, the peninsula so often detested by him, and of which the seer has said: 'It's the land where Larmor must accomplish his redemption'? What is he, then, that man? Oh, how many times, back there in Dublin, in our house on Sackville Street, has he not described these places? And yet, he has never, ever seen them!"

"Lies," the woman interjected, shrugging her shoulders. "He has doubtless visited them, during the war in France, when, in his mad stupidity, he quit his homeland to go and fight under a flag that isn't his own."

"No! He hasn't seen them," said the man, forceful. "When he came to France I was with him, for everywhere he goes, reluctantly, I go. He hadn't seen them, for he said: 'I forbid you to see them before the time,'"

They both remained silent for a moment. The Breton *hroal* was agitating frenziedly, and the dancers were howling their refrain:

> *My love receives my letters.*
> *From the skylark of the fields;*
> *And she sends me hers*
> *By the singing nightingale.*

"Harris," asked the woman, slowly, "why, since you love me, don't you hate *him*?"

"He was my benefactor," replied the man. "He's my father . . . don't look at me like that, darling, oh, not like that! Oh, Bella before you arrived under our roof, I loved him so much! Why are you obliging me to repeat here what I've confided to you so often? Can I forget that he extracted me from the most abject poverty? Yes, yes, I was stagnating in the most abject poverty, and yet Harris O'Riordan, it appears, is of a noble race. My parents were dead and I had been confided, an abandoned waif, to a drunkard, a vagabond accustomed to the workhouse. My God, how I can still remember the day—a winter day of snow and ice—when he came into our hovel on Bathurst Lane in the Liberty district. My companion was lying dead drunk in a corner, and I had just stolen! Suddenly, the door opened; it was *him*! Without pronouncing a word, he walked straight toward me, contemplated me for a long time in silence, put his hand on my head and exclaimed: 'Poor, poor child, I've been searching for you for a long time!" I went with him. Who was he? I didn't know, and no one has ever been able to tell me. And I became his son, better still, his disciple. He taught me the Great Science; he revealed the terrible secret to me, the secret of life and death. Hate him? Bella . . . hate him, who has been so good to me!"

"And to me too," said the woman, angrily. "To me too—and that's why I hate him! Yes, he's been good to Bella. He picked me up too, miserable and famished, in a hovel in our city. In those days, my mother, my own mother, wanted to traffic her daughter and sell my flesh publicly. Well, she was hungry, my mother, and so was I. You're making a gesture of disgust, Harris? Well, *he* married me, the imbecile!"

She interrupted herself to utter a nervous laugh.

"He married me! Oh, truly, perhaps I ought to owe him gratitude! Gratitude? But who else but a starveling like me would have accepted him as a husband, that atheist, that somnambulist, that evoker of the dead, that damned soul who bears the stigma of Hell on his forehead? Gratitude? But since he loved me! Does a woman owe gratitude to all those who love her? Yes, certainly, he was good to me, and yet I hate him! Oh God, I hate him . . . as much, my Harris, as I adore you!"

And the woman brought the man's face toward her own, and I saw them kiss for a long time.

The singers of the hroal where still howling their refrain while dancing:

> *Not knowing how to read or write,*
> *We read what is within,*
> *There is within those letters:*
> *Love me, I love you so much!*

"You swore," the woman said, breaking the silence again, "you swore, Harris, on the eve of our departure . . . I've quit Ireland, a slave of that reprobate, and I only want to return there free . . . oh, to be free, and to be able to love one another without constraint and without remorse!"

"Without remorse!" said the man, in a dolorous tone.

They drew away together.

I saw them in the night, walking slowly, stopping, exchanging a kiss, and slowly walking on. Now they fell silent, holding one another tightly.

"Tomorrow!" said the woman, one last time.

And in an indistinct murmur, it seemed to me that the man replied: "Tomorrow."

IV

. . . .

The place that souls take pleasure in haunting, the man had said, the heathland where the dead can converse with the living. And a voice spoken within me, and said:

"Dare to see!"

. . . .

V

. . . .

The heath of Kermario extended into the distance, solitary; no human sound traversed the immensity of its silence. The night was hot—a blue-tinted night not variegated by any cloud; and in the profundities of the sky, stars scintillated in millions. No breath of wind passed over the plain; the gorse was motionless; nature entire was annihilated in a heavy slumber . . .

And looming up, seemingly sprung from the heather, stood the enormous menhirs, black against the luminous yellow of the flowers of the heath . . . and their lines stretched away as far as the eye could see, plunging fantastically into the distant mysterious mists.

For a long time, already, I had been contemplating the desolation of that solitude, listening to the great voice of the silence. Time went by. In the distance, the clock of Carnac chimed eleven. Almost immediately, toward the east, a glow lit up the horizon: the moon was rising. I started walking in order to return to the village, but the same voice in my heart that had said: "Go!" cried "Stay!"

I stayed.

Suddenly, from a farm lost on the heath, the whining of a dog rose into the air. Oh, the frightful sound, the dolorous plaint! How it was exhaled, sometimes muted, sometimes vibrant. How it was stretched out, lamentably, as it traversed space: the dog was howling mortally.

A frisson ran over my flesh.

The moon emerged then from the abyss of the horizon, spreading its whiteness over the ferns. Ah! A cry was strangled in my throat. There! There, before me, stood a man: a man exactly similar to some corpse rejected by the tomb; the pale rays of moonlight enveloped him like a shroud.

It was a man who was still young, but no one could have specified his age. His proud and arrogant features, his tall stature and the masculine breadth of his shoulders all denounced power and strength. Long black hair framed a beardless face—and so pale, so frightfully pale! His eyes, sunk in their orbits, were shining in the night; they were staring into the void.

Standing on a fallen menhir, the man remained motionless. Sometimes, a convulsive sigh lifted his breast, and his head immediately inclined, as if under the burden of an excessively heavy despair. Sometimes, too, he raised his hand swiftly to his forehead, and a cry of dolor escaped his lips. Then, when he parted his fingers, I thought I glimpsed, traversing his forehead, two red scars, exactly similar to tears, and also similar to two bloodstains . . .

And the hour fled, and the minutes of time fell into eternity one by one . . .

Finally, he broke the silence, and his voice reached me.

"Come," he said. "Oh, come, you who, in the circle of human existences, have known me, have loved me . . . you who are no more, and who are forever . . . you who, traversing death, have attained life . . . O too fortunate survivor of the proof, victor of the three victories, vanquishers by Science, by Amour and by Strength, of my brethren, come to me: I am reaching the end of my pilgrimage, and I am afraid!"

Fearful, chilled by terror, I had collected myself, and, crouched on the ground, hidden in the shadow of a menhir, I extended my head in order to see. From all points of the heath, were demons about to surge? Like a flock of birds, were the dead racing from the profundities of space, about to descend upon us?

But no; no murmur traversed the night, no breath of wind caused the heather to undulate. And yet, they must all have been there—yes, all of them, for the evoker went on:

"Tomorrow! Oh, tomorrow . . . ! Tomorrow, the anniversary of my crime and the term fixed for my expiation! Tomorrow, suffering wringing my heart and the death-rattle choking in my throat! Tomorrow, cold, stupor and annihilation! And tomorrow, the distant gleam, the increasing glow, the dazzle! Terror! Terror! What will be the sentence pronounced when, launching myself into the Night and wanting to plunge myself in the Light, I shall cry: 'I too have submitted to my redemption, I too am purified!'"

He fell silent, and the silent voices doubtless replied to him; then his speech became bitter

"Yes, I know; my crime was horrible, my sin infamous; but I have expiated, for I have suffered; O God, I have suffered . . . !"

And again, his lamentable sigh rose toward the sky.

"I have expiated," he cried, forcefully, "for I love and am not loved! I have expiated, for I am outraged and I refuse to chastise the outrage! I have expiated, for I hate, and I, the stronger, am not avenged!"

His face, contracted now, had become malevolent, and like the eyes of wild beasts, his eyes shone in the night. Soon, however, he seemed to calm down, like a child whom a softly murmured refrain lulls into somnolence, and then to sleep. A strange prostration took possession of him; his head inclined, resignedly.

"Alas, alas!" he said, again.

. . . .

Suddenly—had he perceived me?—he extended his finger toward me, and, terribly:

"Get away from here, sacrilege! Get back, you who have come to surprise the secret of my weakness and my cowardice!"

And abruptly rising to my feet, I started running, and I fled.

VI

The absurd dream!

Six o'clock in the morning chimed; the sunlight came in, bright and warm, through the window of my loft; I leapt out of bed, dressed in haste and went downstairs. In the kitchen of the inn, Madame Lautrem was already busy around her ovens, aided by the two maidservants with white bonnets.

"Hurry up, Monsieur," said the old innkeeper. "Monsieur Gestas has been informed; I'll introduce you to him."

At the same time, she opened a door and went into the dining room adjacent to the kitchen. I stopped on the threshold. In one of the corners of the room, three people were sitting around a pot of tea: two men wearing the costume of English clergymen and a woman clad in black.

"Monsieur Longchamp?" said one of the men, rising to his feet.

He headed toward me, and I remained motionless, as if petrified. I had just recognized the man on the heath, the evoker of souls. Yes, it really was the same person, with his black hair, his pale face and the two red scars traversing his forehead.

Without remarking my stupor, however, he said: "Monsieur Longchamp, the eminent archeologist, the author of the *Essay on the Bardic Triads*?"

I bowed, modest in appearance, although secretly committing the sin of pride.

"Be welcome," Monsieur Gestas continued, extending his hand to me.

Shall I confess it? I did not take it without a certain repugnance. What stupidity, though! It was, in truth, the hand of a man, an amiable and charming man, who had read my work, and who rendered me full justice.

"Be welcome," he said to me, for a second time, and, still holding my hand in his: "It's a long time, Monsieur, such a long time, that I've been waiting for you."

I looked at him in surprise, and swiftly disengaged my fingers from his grip. He did not even seem to perceive my abrupt movement.

"I'll introduce you to my wife," he said, smiling.

Then, turning to the lady sitting in a corner of the room: "Bella! Monsieur Longchamp, a friend of mine, known without him knowing me."

At the name Bella I could scarcely suppress a shudder; and while she looked at me with a disdainful moue, I studied her physiognomy. The woman might have been about twenty-five years old; her mat complexion, her chestnut-colored hair, and the large dark blue eyes illuminating her face all indicated her Irish origin. She lowered her head slightly, without addressing a single word to me.

"And this, my dear friend," Monsieur Gestas continued, still smiling, "is Harris O'Riordan, my adoptive child."

He pronounced the three words "my adoptive child" in a slow voice.

Bella launched a strange glance at her husband. Harris O'Riordan, a man of about thirty, with pink cheeks, clear gray eyes and pale blond hair, saluted me coldly.

"Now," said Monsieur Gestas, "let's go!"

And as we crossed the threshold, he added, talking to himself: "The announced witness has come; the pilgrimage begins."

Two Bretons in Sunday costume were waiting at the door of the hotel.

"Here are the boatmen," said Madame Lautrem, designating them.

They came toward us, and, taking off their broad-brimmed hats, bowed respectfully.

"Does Monsieur Gestas recognize me?" said the first of the men. "Léonnec . . . Jean-Paul Léonnec?"

"And me," said the second. "Little Corant . . . Corant of Ploermel."

Gestas looked at them. "Where have I met you, my friends?"

Léonnec started to laugh. "At the battle of Le Mans, of course, near the bridge over the Huisne. It was there that the shells burst and thundered! What misery! I was next to you. Oh, good God, you didn't have cold in your eyes. You said to us: 'Look death in the face, then; she'll be afraid!' Afraid? The slut! Bah, but in seeing you, a foreigner, fighting for France better than us, Frenchmen, I felt a great shame entering my heart. I was a coward, I became brave, Monsieur Gestas, you taught me to love the fatherland; I bless you."

"Right," said the second of the men in his turn, "and I too was in that bullet storm. It's there that I knew you, my dear Monsieur. German lead had put me down; I was howling in pain and appealing to the comrades. Faint hearts, the comrades! They had other things to do than listen to little Corant; they were running as fast as their legs could carry them. Only you heard me; you lifted me in your arms and loaded me on your shoulders; without you, old Mother Annette would no longer have a son. Monsieur Gestas, you taught me to love humanity; I bless you."

Gestas bowed, and replied, simply: "May I also teach you to love my God!"

We set forth.

"So," I said in my turn, "you were in Le Mans on that lamentable day?"

"Yes," he replied. "At the first news of the disasters in France, I quit Ireland in order to come and fight in your ranks. Oh, don't admire that; I had an imperious duty to do, but I could only arrive to witness the supreme defeat. Alas! Why did I not die that day? But no, the proof would have been too mild."

In silence, we followed the road that led to the beach. The two boatmen marched ahead, conversing in low voices; then came Gestas and me; behind us, Harris and Bella, both going at the tranquil pace of lovers who want to linger. Gestas was somber and taciturn. A nervous movement agitated him; sometimes he stopped abruptly, and immediately resumed walking just as abruptly. He did not turn his head once.

"And you have dared, Monsieur Savant," he suddenly said to me, "to write the sentence: *you alone are my God, you who, by expiation, constrain human beings to become gods!*"

"Certainly," I replied, "but long before me, and much better, the Druids, the first adepts of the Great Science, had said: 'Three things are necessary for the triumph of humankind: to suffer, to change and to choose.'"

"To suffer, to change and to choose," Gestas repeated slowly, in a tremulous voice.

"Yes, the formula of all redemption."

"Oh, redemption!" he exclaimed, dolorously.

A fugitive blush reddened his face, and he raised his hand swiftly to the two stains on his forehead.

VII

The heat was already overwhelming. No breeze traversed the heavy and inflamed air. The sea extended, a transparent blue, flat and polished, devoid of undulations and devoid of ripples.

"We can't hoist the sail," said Léonnec, the owner of the boat. "We'll have to row. Let's go!"

And, bending over the oars, the two boatmen began to beat the water in cadence.

Harris O'Riordan and Bella were sitting next to one another at the rear of the boat. I was not far away, and standing at the prow, Gestas, his head bare and his arms folded, was gazing. We were all silent.

The landscape was superb. To the left was the little isle of Houat, with its girdle of reefs, which the unfurling waves fringed with foam; in front of us, in the distant blue-tinted mists, Belle Isle seemed to be striping the horizon; to the right, flat, yellow and devastated, stretched the peninsula of Quiberon. Here and there, however, between its dunes, patches of dark green showed: a few stunted firs, which the great winter wind had curbed, twisted and tortured.

"In those days," said Gestas, breaking the silence, "those trees didn't even exist."

"They were planted not long ago," replied Léonnec, "but they weren't able to grow."

"Nothing will ever be able to grow on that accursed land," murmured Gestas. "Never, never!"

Again he fell silent. The boatmen were rowing laboriously; somnolence overtook me; Harris and Bella were smiling at one another; and Gestas was still at the prow, gazing.

"Patron," said little Corant to his companion, "the oar's becoming heavy; we're no longer going together. Sing something that will put us back in rhythm."

And Léonnec started to sing, on three notes, a monotonous ballad in the Morbihanese Breton that the purists of Quimper call a dialect, and which I proclaim, myself as the primitive Breton. That *complainte* was curious, even bizarre, and I listened.

"Alleluia! From Auray to Pontivy the bells have rung, and from Auray to Hennebont they are ringing still. And you, lads, come out of your houses, ask for scythes, unhook the carbine and bite the bullet: the beloved hour has come, the hour of battle. *De profundis.*"

"What is that complainte?" I asked. "It certainly isn't in the *Barzaz Breiz.*"[1]

"I can't tell you, Monsieur," replied Léonnec. "My father, formerly of the village of La Trinité, sang it, and his father, it appears, also sang it. I don't know any more."

He continued:

"Alleluia! The beloved hour has come, the hour of battle. And they are gathered, quivering with anger, on the vast heath of Elven. Georges is in the midst of them, and they surround him, for the moment has come to chastise the insolent Gaul, the infamous Blues, the men who drink the blood of men as the drunkard drinks cider. The holy rectors and the good priests are there too; they have blessed the arms; the Breton who dies in these battles will go straight to paradise. *De profundis.*"

An abrupt movement had made the boat oscillate; Gestas had turned round violently, and he was staring at the singer with bleak eyes.[2]

---

1 *Barzaz Breiz* [Breton Bards] (1839) is a collection of ballads and legends, in Breton with French translations, assembled by Théodore Hersart de Villemarqué, which achieved a great success within the context of the Romantic Movement, much as Iolo Morganwg's triads and James Macpherson's Ossianic poems had in the British Isles; like them, its authenticity is nowadays reckoned to be highly dubious.

2 Many readers, like Gestas, would have realized almost immediately that the references in the fictitious ballad are to the Battle of Quiberon in 1795, when émigrés returning from Britain joined Royalist "Chouan" troops under the command of Joseph de Puisaye, in the hope of launching a counter-Revolution. The English ships began disembarking troops on 27 June in the vicinity of Fort Penthièvre. The fort was betrayed to the Republican forces of Lazare Hoche on 20 July—by whom is unknown—and 6,000 Chouans were taken

"Alleluia!" Léonnec went on. "The Breton who dies in these battles will go straight to Paradise. Georges has spoken to them.[1] 'Sons! The ships from England are coming to save us, ships in which all the brave have taken their places, all the knights, all your noblemen: O'Riordan, who was never afraid, Larmor the loyal, who . . .'"

"Larmor was nothing but a wretch," Gestas interjected, dully. "Let his name disappear from history, as his bones will be rejected from the tomb this evening!"

The silence became profound, crushing and strange again. We were advancing very slowly. In the distance, above Belle Isle, a small white cloud was rising, brightly, into the somber blue of the sky.

"We'll have a storm before nightfall," said Léonnec, who, leaning on his oar, resumed his *complainte* mechanically:

"Alleluia! There they are, swaying on their anchors, the ships come from England, the great black and white ships with gleaming canons. Jesus and Mary, here they are at last! To sea, to sea, the boat that will disembark the brave! And Puisaye said: 'The bravest is the man who touches land first.' O'Riordan replied: 'That will be me.' But already, Larmor has thrown himself into the waves, Larmor the loyal . . ."

"Shut up! Oh, shut up, then!" cried Gestas; and seizing the boatman's arm, he twisted it violently.

Bella stood up and, pointing at her husband, said: "That man is mad!"

"No," said Harris, as white as a shroud. "He can see!"

Gestas collapsed heavily on to his bench. His face plunged in his hands, he was silent, and I heard his labored respiration.

prisoner; instead of being treated as prisoners of war, 750 Royalist soldiers, including 430 noblemen, were executed as traitors by a Revolutionary Tribunal headed by Jean-Lambert Tallien. An expiatory chapel was built on the so-called Champ de Martyrs in 1829, and the Chartreuse [i.e., Charterhouse] d'Auray kept the remains of 952 men in a vault, with a list of their names.

1 "Georges" was the customary appellation of the Chouan leader Georges Cadoudal.

I touched his shoulder. "Monsieur, what is that man singing, then?" I dared to ask.

Then, letting his arms fall back, he replied to me in a harsh voice: "The legend of Quiberon."

VIII

The boat felt a slight shock; it had just touched the bottom; but only a few brasses separated us from the shore, and the tide was going out rapidly. In front of us, a little sandy cove extended, its yellow dunes dotted with black granite. To the left, a redoubt that had almost collapsed, the southern fort, allowed the mouths of a few old cannons to be glimpsed behind its parapet; to the right, the hamlet of Port Haliguen scattered its houses along the shore.

"It's here!" said Gestas, shaking off his torpor. "Here! Eighty years, already!"

He gave the impression of struggling against a will superior to his own, but, as if vanquished in that interior combat, he said:

"Listen, Harris, and understand! Larmor was cleaving the waves, racing toward the shore, in order to be first to land. A hand posed on his shoulder: O'Riordan was beside him, looking at him . . . as you're looking at me, at this moment. He was noble, very noble, Earl O'Riordan, from an Irish family that had taken refuge in France with James II, but no less noble as him was Baron Larmor, of the Larmors who were killed in the Crusades. Both of them, officers of the king, lived in neighboring seigneuries: O'Riordan in the château that you can see over to the right, lost in the heather, on the slope descending to the river at Auray; Larmor in that old lair whose disemboweled tower can still be seen on the coast of Morbihan, amid the black fir trees and the great somber oaks. Oh, how desolately the winter wind moans as it passes over those enormous forests, curbing them. How lugubriously the flocks of crows croak, in the days of Autumn, around those solitary ruins!

"And both of them were brave, very brave, Baron Larmor and Earl O'Riordan. It was already three years since they had emigrated, respiring the hatred of their homeland for three years. Now they were disembarking on the coast of France in order to cut French throats, wearing English coats with pockets stuffed with English pounds. Oh, woe to the sacrilege that cannot love you, you whose soil is made with the dust of our forefathers, you who receive the imprint of the first footprints of our children, twice sacred thing, great family, powerful mother, Homeland!"

I had drawn closer to Gestas and I contemplated him, almost with terror, that Seer for whom the past was so very present, that living man who was reviving the lives of the dead. Only Bella had remained seated, and, with a smile of disdain on her lips, she was tapping the planks of the boat with her umbrella.

Gestas went on:

"'Larmor,' said O'Riordan, tugging his arm, 'I hate you.'

"Larmor shrugged his shoulders.

"'Yes, I hate you, the earl went on, 'and again, you're going to steal my share of glory!'

"Larmor started to snigger, and thought: *Your share of glory, as I've already stolen your share of love, your allotment of happiness!*

"'One of the two of us,' said O'Riordan, 'is surplus to requirements; that one must disappear.'

"Larmor still kept quiet, but he thought: *It will be you.* An infamous idea had just sprung forth in his mind.

"Come," Gestas commanded, speaking rudely to Harris. "It's necessary, finally, that you know."

Then, leaping out of the boat, he started running toward the strand.

"Harris," said Bella, retaining the young man by the hand. "Earl O'Riordan, you have sworn!"

She drew closer to him, and whispered to him very quietly, two words in English:

"This evening."

[At this point the manuscript is interrupted; several pages left blank cut the text; then the story resumes.]

IX

. . . .

And we went.

"Giddy up! Giddy up!"

The driver whipped his beast with a sweep of his arm. The little Breton horse shook its head angrily and increased its pace. The cart made an enormous leap, and all four of us were shaken by rude jolts. What a strange equipage—the only one that we had been able to find in the village of Port Haliguen!

"Giddy up! Giddy up!"

Gestas had said to the innkeeper: "First, to the hamlet of Lenneiz; then to Fort Penthièvre; finally, to the Chartreuse d'Auray."

The innkeeper, while drinking his coffee laced with brandy, his "little tipple," had replied: "Today, August the second, daylight lasts until eight o'clock, so all that can be done, but you won't arrive before the storm . . ."

"Giddy up! Giddy up!"

The horse ran, flat out, and the landscapes succeeded one another rapidly before our eyes. Behind us, already, the town of Quiberon and its tall square clock-tower; to the right, now, the village of Saint-Pierre and its menhirs . . . oh, old and dear friends, you whom I had come to see again, was it thus that I was keeping the promise made to myself? But no, I was scarcely thinking about you; I too wanted to know what this Larmor was.

"Giddy up! Giddy up!"

The heath . . . the heath . . . the heath, with its spiny gorse, its green ferns and its variegation of pink heather and yellow flowers . . . the heath! Oh, what charms there are in your desolation! What beauty there is in your ugliness, earth of great poetry, Bretagne!

"Giddy up! Giddy up!"

The little white cloud that had been floating, that morning, above Belle Isle, was now spread out over our heads, black, sinister and concealing the storm. The wind was beginning to blow. To the right, the waves of the bay were splashing against the shore; to the left, the ocean, the "savage sea" was twisting its waves over the reefs and silvering with foam. Out there, at sea, the "howlers' reef" was replete with sobs.

"Giddy up! Giddy up!"

We had traversed the peninsula in its full length. At the place where a tongue of land soldered it to the continent, on a hill of sand and mud, stood a house . . .

"Stop!" commanded Gestas; and he was the first of us to leap to the ground.

X

It was a house of solid appearance, with cob walls slit by zigzag cracks, a thatched roof caved in and eaten way by moss. For a long time, no doubt, it had stood thus, solitary on the dune, and for a long time, the March winds and the November gales had harassed it with their bites and battered it with their swirls. A low wall of dry stones formed a narrow enclosure in which a few ears of buckwheat with glabrous flowers grew, undulating at the slightest wind. Outside the door, a dung-heap emitted its vapors and allowed a nauseating liquid manure to leak out, drop by drop. All that spoke of abandonment; all of it also reeked of poverty and hunger.

Gestas went into the enclosure. Suddenly, a dog crouching against the house got up and bounded toward us: one of those big sheepdogs with short hair, bloodshot eyes and enormous fangs . . . but it stopped dead, lay down on its belly, and started trembling in every limb. Gestas marched slowly toward the house. Then the dog started recoiling before him, step by step, uttering continuous dolorous howls—the same frightful plaint that I had heard the evening before in the silence of the heathland of Kermario. Harris, still very pale, picked up a stone and wanted to throw it at the dog.

"He won't shut up," said Bella, curling her lip in disgust, "he's sniffed a cadaver!"

The door was closed on the outside by a latch. Gestas opened it, and closed it behind us.

The interior of the abode was truly filthy. A single room formed the entire habitation. The beaten earth that took the place of floorboards was hollowed out by rain dripping from the roof on stormy days. On the walls, once whitewashed, smoke and dust spread large patches. A table scarred in many places by a knife and a few rickety stools were the entire furniture of the sordid redoubt. In a corner of the room, a bed seemed to be embedded in the wall—a Breton bed in the form of a cupboard, with crude sculptures, in worm-eaten wood. Two ragged calico curtains, closed off the bed. The daylight, already darkening outside, had difficulty filtering through the only dusty and greasy window; it was almost dark in the hovel . . .

No one!

Suddenly, a human voice similar to a death-rattle spoke in a corner of the room:

"The traitor! The traitor!"

Immediately, the red calico curtains agitated, and then opened, and a man appeared in the gloom, sitting on the bed: a tall old man of almost centenarian appearance. Long greenish-gray hair fell over his shoulders; the hairs of a white beard garnished the cavities of his cheeks in clumps; the rictus of his mouth allowed the sight of gums devoid of teeth; two large white leucomas extended over his eyes: the old man was blind. He extended a tremulous finger toward us and spoke for the second time:

"The traitor! The traitor!" he murmured.

Gestas marched toward the old man and placed his hand on his shoulder. "Yes, yes," he said, "eighty years have already been accomplished." And, in a tone of profound melancholy: "In those days, you entered into life in pain; and now you're about to leave it . . . from infancy you've returned to infancy."

"The traitor!" stammered the man sitting on the bed, for the third time, and bizarre words, phrases devoid of meaning, emerged in hiccups from the lips of the miserable idiot.

"General Hoche is here," he said, "sitting over there!" With his finger he pointed to a long Breton coffer placed near the bed. "At his side, the man who arrived yesterday has taken his place, the man with long hair, the man with the tricolor sash, the man of the Convention. Oh, sweet Jesus! Holy Virgin! What's going to happen? The general gets up . . . he's marching angrily.

"'No capitulation, then?'

"'No capitulation!' replies the man with the sash.

"'And everyone, everyone has passed under arms?'"

"'Passed under arms,' replies the man, again.

"Me, I look at my mother, on her knees beside the fireplace, preparing a meal. She's weeping. This morning, Father disappeared. He's gone to join the others, out there . . .

"The general stops again and says: 'For a fortnight, the émigrés have been masters of Fort Penthièvre; they're retrenched there; to take the fort will be hard.'

"'The fort will be taken,' says the man with the sash, simply . . .

"*Pif! Paf!* Rifle shots. 'What's that?'

"An aide-de-camp rushes outside and comes back immediately. 'They've just captured a clown who was prowling around the house. He wants to speak to you urgently.'

"'Send him in.'

"Aha! There he is. A large hat is pulled down over his face; he's wearing a jacket and britches like our peasants. The general asks: 'What do you want with me?'

"The peasant replies, and he talks in good French: 'For a fortnight the Whites have been masters of Penthièvre. They're fortified there; you'll be repelled.'

"'Is that all you have to tell me, spy?' cries the general. 'What's your name?'

"The peasant takes off his hat and throws it across the room. 'My name is Claude-Marie, Baron de Larmor.'

"'A former nobleman?'

"'Oh yes, a very former nobleman!'

"'What do you have to tell me?'

"'This. Tonight I'll be guarding the postern that opens over the sea. Are there fifteen hundred brave men among your Republicans?'

"The general shrugs his shoulders. Larmor goes on: 'Well, let them slip along the strand, tonight, as far as that postern, and they'll see what a former nobleman dares to do!'

"The general looks at Larmor suspiciously and interrogates the man in the sash with his eyes. 'And what recompense are you asking from us to pay for your service?'

"Larmor straightens up. 'Keep your recompense! I'm not serving your Republic, I'm serving my hatred!' Then, in a low, sniggering voice: 'O'Riordan is in the fort, and I'm his wife's lover!'

"Then the man in the sash, the silent man, the man of the Convention, Tallien, starts to laugh, and says: 'In that case, Penthièvre is ours!'"

XI

. . . And Fort Penthièvre appeared in the dusk, bleak and somber.

Out at sea, the storm, now unleashed, was raging. Lightning was streaking the horizon; thunder was rumbling dully. To the right and the left of the road, the waves of the bay and the waves of the savage sea were unfurling with a great murmur.

The door of the fort was open; the guardian was doubtless absent; Penthièvre was abandoned to us.

Gestas went in.

On the drawbridge, Harris appeared to hesitate. "Bella," he said, in a low voice, "I'm afraid."

"March," she replied, harshly. "It's necessary that you see."

Beyond the drawbridge, a round-path turned. To the left was a dilapidated barracks, to the right a high wall pierced by loopholes. Gestas set forth along the path.

The path descended in a slope parallel to the ocean and terminated abruptly in a stairway of several steps. At the bottom of the steps was a postern, and behind the postern, the roar of the waves beating the rocks was audible. At that moment, a flash of lightning lit up the night, and for a second we saw, as if in broad daylight, Gestas' livid face, his ardent eyes, and, on his forehead, the two red-brown stains that had surprised me so strangely the previous evening.

Gestas went down the stairs leading to the postern. Like a somnambulist, he went . . . he spoke . . . he listened . . . he heard.

"'Aha! The storm so ardently desired, the storm that will permit them to slip all the way here.' He looks at his watch. 'It's time! They can enter. The guard at the postern is me!'" He made the gesture of opening the door. 'Come on, come on! Hurry up beloved artisans of my hatred!' Here they are . . . they enter . . . they climb up . . .

"'To arms!' The general! The fort is in tumult. 'Too late, wretch, you're doomed!' Ah! An officer of the Loyal Emigrant comes running, lantern in hand. 'Fire! Fire on that one! It's O'Riordan!' He falls . . . is he dead?

"No . . . he's calling out . . . he has recognized . . .

"'Larmor! Larmor, my companion in arms, save me!'

"Larmor approaches, leans over the wounded man. He takes two pistols from his cloak. He leans over again, and discharges his weapons at point-blank range.

"'Ah! Larmor! Infamy . . . '

"And Larmor whispers in his ear: 'Yes, infamy, for it's me who delivered Penthièvre in order that you would die, and that I could return to your wife, your widow, my mistress!'

"Then O'Riordan raises himself up on one elbow; he dips his hand in the blood of his wounds, and two drops of blood have just splashed Larmor's face. 'Larmor, I don't know whether there is a God, but if he exists, may he chastise you, may he chastise you until you have expiated!'"

Exhausted, Gestas fell to the ground, on his knees. Sobs lifted his breast, but he was not weeping . . .

And Bella, approaching, extended her hands over the man's head, and without saying a word to him, but looking hard at Harris, she pointed with her finger at the two stigmata similar to two drops of blood.

For a long time, the three of them remained thus, silent in the midst of the howling of nature in torment.

XII

And our journey over the heath resumed, furiously.

"Giddy up! Giddy up!"

Damn the tempest, which now seems to be pursuing us determinedly! The lightning flashes blind us, the thunder deafens us, the torment shakes us, the rain lashes us.

"Giddy up! Giddy up!"

The night envelops us, thick and black . . .

Out there, in the gray vapors, lights scintillate and tremble. That's Auray.

"Giddy up! Giddy up!"

The vehicle traverses the town. The gallop of the horse strikes sparks from the pavement; the wheels resonate with a strident metallic sound . . .

The houses become rarer; the lights disappear; the heath again. Emerged from night, we reenter night.

"Giddy up! Giddy up!"

Abruptly, we turn left. A long avenue of fir trees extends, utterly funereal. The vehicle stops. In front of us, a little edifice with a Dorian portico.

"That's the ossuary," says the driver, and he makes the sign of the cross.

We get down.

"Go away!" says Gestas to the driver, and throws him a purse.

The other counts the coins by the light of his lantern; he laughs and says: "Thanks! Giddy up! Giddy up!" And the vehicle draws away.

Shivering under the downpour, I listen to the sound decreasing in the darkness. A gust of wind carries a "Giddy up! Giddy up!" to us . . . now, nothing more.

Gestas is still motionless, not daring to cross the threshold of the chapel. Harris looks him up and down.

"Larmor, I don't know whether there is a God, but if he exists, may he chastise you, may he chastise you until you have expiated!"

And the voice of that debilitated being resonates, menacingly.

"Yes, does he exist, that one?" asks Bella, with a cynical laugh.

Then Gestas bows his head. "He exists."

At a slow pace, he climbs the steps of the ossuary.

XIII

The door stood ajar, allowing a ray of light to filter out. Gestas pushed it; it swung on its hinges, without making a sound.

The chapel that we had just entered was an edifice of medium size, with walls sumptuously paneled with marble, the vault of which constellated with fleurs-de-lys; here and there, on the plaster-work, inscriptions stood out in golden letters, taken from the Scriptures. A vast mausoleum in the form of a catafalque occupied the center of the chapel, and a second door, of bronze, gave access to it; it was open. Still preceding us, Gestas slipped into the tomb.

There, a large square pit was gaping, and a ladder permitted descent into it. The smoky light of a lantern was projected over several death's-heads, and those heads seemed to be staring at us with their empty eyes and smiling their eternal smile at us.

Sitting amid that human debris was a nun, a very young woman, doubtless a novice. She was wearing the costume of the Soeurs de la sagesse: the robe of white linen, the white veil, the white wimple. Her pale, emaciated face had ivory reflections, and in the light of the lantern the forehead of that living person was as shiny as the foreheads of the skulls. Beside her was a bucket of water, and the little sister was washing the skulls with a sponge. While she did her repulsive work, thinking that she was alone, she was speaking aloud.

"Yes, yes," she said. "You'll all have your toilette . . . and a hundred!"[1]

She placed a cleaned head among others that were piled up.

"A fine toilette, for tomorrow is your anniversary, your feast day; tomorrow, the Dean of Saint-Gustan will come to say a high mass in your honor. It's necessary to be very clean, very genteel, for that day . . . a hundred and one."

The new head placed on the pile rolled on to the ground. The little sister picked it up.

"Uh oh, Monsieur Mutineer, what's this? You're playing the rebel!"

She took it in both hands and gazed at it pensively.

"Yes, you're my favorite, you. Oh, you must have been pretty, very pretty, once . . . big blue eyes, curly blond hair, a martial air, and doubtless a bad boy . . . a true Saint Michel! And now . . . uh oh! No matter, you're my favorite . . ."

Her hands approached the skull to her face, and her lips extended as if to give the hideous thing a kiss. But her movement stopped dead; she made a rapid sign of the cross, murmuring: "Jesus and Mary . . . !

"A hundred and two," she added, with a sigh, and threw the head among the others. "And you, Monsieur," she said, suddenly,

---

1 The Soeurs oblates de la sagessse, founded in 1859, were a silent order, so this one is a trifle garrulous.

"you who are trying to hide back there, I can see you! Come on, it's necessary to be nice and clean, like the friends. You can look at me with your nasty eyes, I'm not afraid. Oh, you must have been wicked, once!"

She extended her hand and picked up another skull.

Suddenly, Gestas, who was watching all that with haggard eyes, uttered a strangled exclamation. The little sister looked up and perceived us. With an abrupt movement she came to her feet; a blush spread over her face, soon followed by a livid pallor. She was afraid.

"What do you want?" she stammered. "What do you want? Oh yes . . ."—she strove to laugh—"visitors, no doubt? But it's late, much too late!"

Rapidly, she came toward us. "It's much too late. The doors of the chapel close at seven o'clock, and ten o'clock has just chimed . . . ! Anyway, as you're here . . ."

Her teeth were chattering with terror; she could not finish her sentence. She paused, as if to pull herself together

"Madame et Messieurs," she said, in the monotonous tone of a cicerone, "you are in the expiatory chapel constructed in honor of the victims of Quiberon by Her Royal Highness Madame la Duchesse d'Angoulême,[1] and this is the crypt in which their remains are deposited, which remains sacred to the hearts of good Frenchmen, for the heroes of Quiberon died as martyrs for their God and their King. Now, turn your eyes and look. There, inscribed on the mausoleum are the names of the victims, nine hundred and fifty-two names, and among them the most illustrious in France: a Broglie, a Soulanges, a Sombreuil, a Talhouët, a Larmor . . ."

"What is the name of that traitor doing here?" howled Gestas, with a threatening gesture.

---

1 La Duchesse d'Angoulême was the title employed after her marriage to the eldest son of the future Charles X by Marie-Thérèse-Charlotte of France (1778-1851), the eldest daughter of Louis XVI and Marie-Antoinette.

The little sister looked at him fearfully. "You can't stay! You can't stay!" she stammered. "Leave!"

Gestas had approached the ladder and had already put his foot on a rung. Then, uttering a cry of fright, the little sister ran outside.

. . . .

"And that, I have seen, yes, I've seen it!"

Gestas let himself fall into the tomb, took possession of the head that the nun had been holding, and uttered a strident laugh.

"It's him! Him, Larmor!"

He came back up, holding the skull between his arms.

I tried to stop him.

"Infamous sacrilege, Monsieur! Horrible sacrilege!"

But he pointed at one of the inscriptions traced on the wall, and I read:

My bones like grass will germinate and be reborn.

XIV

And he went on, he went on . . .

The rain had stopped, but in the tormented sky great clouds were running, the gaps in which allowed momentary glimpses of a large crescent moon. Sometimes its rays, falling obliquely, spread a mat whiteness over the gorse and the heather; sometimes plunged to shadow again, the heather and the gorse resumed their sinister coloration.

And he went on, and on . . .

With his folded arms he pressed the skull stolen from the tomb against his breast.

The path descended steeply, muddy and eroded by the rain, an escarpment bristling with broom; to the left was a profound ravine where a stream swollen by the rain was howling, rolling from one waterfall to the next. To either side, mossy oaks with rugged trunks extended their branches toward us, as if in a gesture of menace.

And he went on, and on . . .

At the bottom of the slope, a stone cross barred the way. Gestas went around it and engaged in a long path of funerary pines that bordered an immense heath. In the middle of that heath a river ran, which the rising tide was driving back with little splashes. In the moonlight, that marsh, cut by pools of water, shone and scintillated. A lugubrious silence weighed upon the place; the desolation of the solitude extended as far as the eye could see . . .

And yet, from the distance, but very far away, the sound of human labor reached us. The river was dammed; a mill was rumbling slowly, and a red dot of light shone in the night. Out there, in the midst of that reposed and slumbering nature, a man was awake, a man was working.

Gestas stopped at the foot of a fir tree; he sat down.

We were grouped around him, Bella leaning impudently on Harris's arm.

"Larmor!" said Gestas, speaking to the skull that he was holding in both hands. "It is eighty years since, on this heath of Brech, more than nine hundred of your armed companions fell under the bullets. Traitors had delivered them, and you were the most infamous among those traitors.

"Larmor! It is eighty years since, on this heath of Brech, you too fell under the bullets. Captured with the others and clad in the royalist uniform, you were put before the council of war. Tallien refused to recognize you, and when you implored him he started to laugh. Had you not said: 'I'm not serving your Republic, I'm serving my hatred!' You had your recompense. That day, you, the skeptic, the atheist, died blaspheming, for you had just learned that a God exists . . .

"And for a very long time, Larmor, the voice of the One who chastises as recompenses has been speaking to me and saying to me: 'Go out there, to the land where your crime was accomplished; take from the glories of his tomb the bones of the unworthy, and disperse them in the same place where he expiated the first time—for it is there that he must expiate again . . .'

"I am obeying."

Then, getting to his feet, Gestas threw into the mud of the heath the last remaining bone of Claude-Marie, Baron de Larmor.

There was a long silence.

Finally, Gestas said, in a dull voice: "The pilgrimage is terminated. The expiation is accomplished."

But he was speaking in an ill-assured tone, like a man who does not really believe what he is affirming.

Harris placed a hand on his shoulder.

For a long time, the two of them looked one another in the face. They were not speaking, and yet they were listening; they understood one another.

With an imperious movement, the master pushed away his disciple's arm, and seized his hands in his own.

"Oh! Oh! Truly, Larmor has not expiated sufficiently? And it's you who dare to think so . . . you! You!"

He extended his finger toward Bella. "Larmor has not expiated sufficiently? Look at that woman, and dare to tell me that!"

"You know, then?" stammered the young man. You know . . ."

Gestas, raising his clenched fists and letting them fall back, was terrible. "I know that I could have crushed both of you!"

"Harris!" cried Bella, clinging to her lover. "Defend me and avenge yourself!"

He pushed her away gently; then, after a brief silence, he said: "Gestas, what O'Riordan, my ancestor, said to Larmor, I say to you: 'One of the two of us is surplus to requirements. Do you understand? Listen. The O'Riordans are not assassins, so it's a duel that I offer you, a duel without mercy, but honest. Are you ready?"

From the pockets of his cloak he drew two revolvers, gripped one of them, and held out the other.

"Give!" And Gestas, taking possession of the revolver, armed himself.

They stood facing one another, six meters apart, taking aim, ready to fire.

"You're the elder," said Harris, "begin!"

But Gestas raised his arm; the flame of anger that had illuminated his face had just gone out.

"No," he said, in a very soft voice. "I won't kill my son . . ."

"His son!" howled the young man, with a laugh full of rage. "Fire, then!"

"No," replied the new Gestas. "I won't kill O'Riordan." He dropped his weapon and kicked it away. Then, his eyes fixed his challenger, he marched toward him. "I won't kill the executor of the sentence."

Then, as if the master's gaze had twisted his wrist, Harris dropped the revolver.

But suddenly, with a rapid bound, Bella leapt forward, bent down, and picked up the weapon.

"Harris!" she cried. "Cowardly heart, which cannot love to the point of crime!"

Three times, at point-blank range, she fired at her husband.

Gestas fell.

"Her . . . her!" he murmured. "So she is the executor of the sentence."

And he lost consciousness.

I ran toward him, and with loud cries, I called for help.

At the extremity of the heath, in the distance, in the direction of the mill, a light passed back and forth in the night; a rumor reached us. Someone had heard me.

Stupefied, Harris stood still, nailed to the ground. Bella approached the young man and, offering him her hand, only pronounced one word: "Finally."

Suddenly, as if revived by the sound of that beloved voice, the moribund man made a movement and opened his eyes. "Bella! My Bella?" he asked.

She clasped her lover more tightly.

"Oh, the poor woman!" stammered Gestas.

From the depths of the heath, lights advanced toward us, and cries drew nearer.

"What's that?" asked the wounded man.

"Help, Monsieur," I replied. "It's coming."

Then a bizarre change, a mysterious transformation, was operated in that man, almost dead already. His halting respiration became regular again; for a moment, the death-rattle ceased to strangle his throat.

Gestas freed himself from my grip and leaned back against a tree

"Harris, and you, Bella, go!" he commanded in a forceful voice. "Go, both of you, there's still time. Monsieur"—he designated me—"will attest that I committed suicide. Go back to the house in Dublin; you'll find my will there, which makes you the heirs of my petty estate. I forgive! One more word: your first-born will bear my name, and him too you will educate in the Great Science. I wish it! Now, come closer, my son."

Harris seemed to be struggling with himself, but, like a somnambulist. He advanced slowly and knelt down.

Gestas ran his hand over the forehead and then the eyes of his disciple.

"Harris," he said, affectionately, "in your hours of weakness and despair—they will be numerous for you, those hours, poor feeble heart—often, you will feel the same caress that your dying father is giving you. You will know then that old Gestas is nearby. Now, go!"

"Come on, Harris," said Bella, brutally.

They both drew away, rapidly.

Gestas raised himself up on his elbow. I supported his head, and silently he watched them draw away. At a bend in the path, Harris and Bella disappeared.

"She didn't even turn her head," said the dying man. "No matter. May she be happy. I forgive." Then, suddenly, and joyfully:

"What! I'm weeping—me, who didn't know until today what a tear is! The redemption of amour is, therefore, accomplished by amour. Gestas has redeemed Larmor."

Here the manuscript of the archeologist Longchamp ends. Nevertheless, at the bottom of the last page, my savant friend had written this comment:

> *Gestas buried in the cemetery of the little parish of Larmor, near Auray. No name on the tomb, but this text from the triads:*
> *Three victories redeem anterior and evil humanity: Science, Love and Strength.*

No other explanation was given by the author of this bizarre story, so full of incomprehensible strangeness. And yet, I closed the manuscript very troubled. I remained pensive for a long time.

REDIVIVA

Eva

I

May 185*

My friend, Doctor Marcus, emerged from the room where Eva was sleeping; I followed him. Slowly, he went down the staircase of the château, and went silently to lean on the balusters of the terrace.

Dusk was falling. Below us, at the bottom of the hill, the town of Vauvilliers, with its gray houses and its red roofs, appeared flamboyant in the blaze of the setting sun; in front of us, the hills of Faucilles, black with woods, licked the plain with their immeasurable shadow; and further away, over the "balloons" of Alsace, in the pearly vapors, the first stars were already showing, pale and seemingly fearful. A few more moments, and one of the earth's days would sink into the past of worlds.

I broke the silence first.

"Well, Marcus, what do you think of the unfortunate Eva?"

He turned round and looked me straight in the face.

"Be happy, Monsieur de Tréan. Eva will not see tomorrow's dawn shine."

Marcus was no longer addressing me familiarly; his face was hard and his lips were tremulous with anger. He seized my arm, and said, in a dull voice: "Be happy; Eva will die tonight. The death-throes have commenced. Oh, that's agreeable news, isn't it true, Monsieur? Tomorrow, your liberty will finally be recovered, and all the life of facile pleasures will be reborn; tomorrow, it's gambling and prostitutes! With what embraces the gallant girls will salute your return, Monsieur debaucher of honest women!"

Insensible, but shrugging my shoulders slightly, I let the flood of unseemly words and banal moralities erupt.

Marcus released my arm and became solemn. "Do you know, Jean, that blood, from now on, will cry out against you . . . Eva's husband is dead."

"What do you mean, dead?" I said, rolling a cigarette.

"He has killed himself. Read."

Marcus took a newspaper from his pocket and held it out to me. In the Parisian news I perceived an item ringed in red pencil, and I read:

> *Very sad news: we have just learned of the death of Monsieur Yves Mériadec. That premature end was due, it seems, to a suicide. The unfortunate man was found yesterday morning lying in his bedroom, lifeless. He had plunged a dagger into his throat. Family chagrin had motivated that fatal determination. A letter that the dead man was holding between his fingers left no doubt in that regard.*
>
> *It is well-known that Yves Mériadec had acquired a certain public notoriety by virtue of his studies in theurgy and spiritism. He was one of the great pontiffs of the Occult. Another poor man whom the omnipotence of the Spirits has not been able to preserve from the petty accidents of humanity!*

"Yes, poor man," I said, tranquilly, returning the newspaper to Doctor Marcus.

"Now," the latter went on, "would you like to know his last adieu and his supreme thought? Listen!" He opened his portfolio, took out a piece of paper, and read me these simple words: "*Eva, I forgive you.*"

In spite of myself, I lowered my head, and a profound silence fell between us.

Marcus spoke again: "The poor woman! To have deserted her duties for the love of a man who is incapable of love!"

I tried to protest, but he went on: "Shut up! You never loved that woman, you who, knowing that she was doomed, only called me in order to confront me with her cadaver. It's all over now. There's nothing I can do but go. Adieu!"

He went down the steps of the perron without me making a gesture to retain him. However, when he reached the last step, the doctor turned round. Was it an effect of the dusk, was it an illusion of my disturbed mind? It seemed to me that his tall stature had increased further. The sun's last rays enveloped him like an aureole, and his long hair and black beard appeared to emit strange reflections.

Marcus extended his arm toward me, and said: "Mériadec, my venerated master, was able to forgive, but the One who hates Evil, because he appeals to the Good, does not forgive thus! Woe betide the two of you, then! Sooner or later it will be necessary for you to expiate, in the Inferno down here—and perhaps for both of you to expiate together . . ."

He left. For a few moments, I saw him going down the winding path that leads to Vauvilliers. Night had fallen, but I could perceive Marcus distinctly in the shadows. He was walking at a feverish pace, stopping, turning round to look behind, and resuming his course. Finally, he disappeared.

The wind from the Vosges had risen, putting shivers into the foliage of the old trees in the park. And again, traversing the murmur of the great chestnut trees, I thought I heard these bizarre words: "Woe betide you, then! Sooner or later, it will be necessary for you to expiate . . . perhaps for both of you to expiate together . . ."

"Had Marcus told the truth? Free—I was free! So, death was bringing the rupture so much desired; it was about to break the chain that weighed more heavily every day upon my twenty-three years . . .

Free . . . ! But also, what a vulgar and stupid adventure! To abduct a woman from her husband, publicly! And who? A petty bourgeoise, the wife of a man who was almost ridiculous. To impose a burden on myself, almost a duty, and to know one's own heart so poorly as to call a simple caprice passion! Oh, how they laughed in society at my sad escapade! What epigrams at my club! What bursts of laughter at the Grand Seize and the Moulin Rouge! Little Vitray had laughed at my simplicity; even Raoul d'Amance, the dearest of my friends, had shrugged his shoulders, and in her old town house in the Rue de Varenne, how my mother had wept over my sin!

Free . . . !

Eva was dying. For twelve hours, a frightful torpor had enchained her limbs, annihilated her thought.

The night had become dense in the bedroom. I lit a candle and approached the bed on which the young woman was lying. For a long time I gazed at her in the tremulous candle-light. I gazed at her long blonde hair spread over the pillow, the motionless large blue eyes, the convulsively clenched lips and the meager cheeks, which two creases hollowed out at the corners of the mouth. The discolored face had taken on an ivory tint, but two tiny pink patches stood out against the mat whiteness of the face above each cheekbone.

Oh, how familiar that sign was to me, where consumption had engraved its imprint. How many times in the hours when I thought I was in love, had my lips posed upon it for a long time, and how many times, too, shivering under that caress had Eva said to me with a heart-rending smile: "Love me well, Jean, for you have so few days to love me . . ."

And I gazed at her, pensively.

I placed the candle on a table near the bed, and, taking a chair, I sat down. On that table there were a few volumes, bizarre books with truly strange titles: Porphyry's *Theurgy*; Iamblichus' *Egyptian Mysteries*; a French translation of the Bardic triads, with commentaries; Swedenborg's *Arcana of Heaven*; and the famous work by Jean Reynaud, *Earth and Heaven.*[1] I riffled through them by turns and pushed them away one by one. I took possession of one last volume, but I shivered suddenly, unable to repress a start of surprise.

It was a pamphlet of a hundred pages, the fatigue and wear of which attested that Eva had read it and meditated upon it many times. The cover bore a single word: *Redemption*, and the book's author was Yves Mériadec . . .

Yves Mériadec, Eva's husband, yesterday's suicide!

I opened the book at random, and I read:

> *And I, too, want to cry to you, O Death: "Where, then, is your victory?" Yes, to die is to be reborn, and to be reborn, to expiate.*
>
> *O law of Redemption by the necessity of reincarnation and the torments of the Inferno of life—implacable and yet merciful law! You are the supreme reason for the moral progress accomplished by humanity. Thanks to you, the fraternity of all men, brethren in death, will one day reign over his poor earth. No more exploitation of poverty, no more monstrous egotism of opulence! Henceforth, the evil rich man will tremble to refuse the crumbs of his table to Lazarus the pauper, since he will know that the dung-heap of Lazarus awaits him in his turn. Thanks to you, again, no more slaughter*

---

1 Jean Reynaud's *Terre et ciel: philosophie religieuse* was first published in 1854, and went through numerous editions thereafter.

by war, no more extermination of men by men! Dare, then, Napoléon, to launch people against the mouths of cannons, if you, an obscure soldier, must fall one day under the bullets and you too are to utter the great cry of thirst on the evening of the battle. Never has a more terrible meaning been given to the words: "Woe betide you who laugh, for you will weep!"

At that point the sick man had underlined a passage and written a few words in pencil in the margin. The book continued, in its mysterious and tormented style:

Amour, life of worlds, you whom the great Being created to become the morality of all beings; you who put happiness into duty and sensual pleasure even into suffering, Amour, who makes the wife, Amour who makes the mother, woe betide those who abuse you!

"Jean," a voice suddenly murmured in my ear, "why have you never loved me?"

I sat up with a start. Eva's hand had settled on my shoulder, and her breath was burning my cheek.

She extended her finger toward the pamphlet. "He loved me so much . . . the man we've betrayed, the man we've killed!"

A tremor agitated her body; she went on, her breathing labored: "Yves Mériadec is dead, Jean, we have killed him. For long hours I've just seen him, there . . . there, beside my bed! He had his eyes fixed on mine; he was very pale, very bloody, and had a hideous wound in his throat. He looked at me for a long time without addressing a single word to me; then, twice, he extended his hand toward my neck. Finally, he disappeared. Jean, he ordered me to follow him. He and I will be summoned to judgment. Oh, I'm afraid! To what punishment of the Inferno of life will I be condemned? Yes, I'm afraid!"

A smile, nevertheless, parted her lips. "And yet, I don't repent, I don't regret anything . . . I've loved!"

She approached her face to mine, and, lowering her voice, spoke so quietly, so quietly that I could not hear . . . and yet, yes, I affirm it, I understood . . .

"Jean, a little more time, and we'll see one another again, doubtless to expiate together and then to love without remorse in the life of space . . ."

Eva placed her hand on my shoulder again. Under that feeble pressure, as if under a crushing burden, I fell to my knees.

"Listen," she said to me, "and remember . . . Wherever on earth you will encounter me, and in whatever human form my soul is clad, this is the sign by which you will recognize me!"

Very slowly, her hand moved over my forehead, my eyes and my lips . . . and suddenly, I felt an atrocious pain that gripped my temples and wrung my heart. I uttered a cry, and she started to laugh.

"Remember!" she said, again.

At that moment, her head slumped. I heard a long sigh; her hand released me, and fell back, rigid. I got up, threw myself upon her and wrapped my arms around her. Her pulse was no longer beating; even the death-rattle had ceased; her face was as white as a shroud, and upon that whiteness, the two roseate patches appeared more visibly . . .

And for two days and two nights I called to her, striving to re-animate her with my kisses, howling in pain, but not weeping.

I was in love . . . I was in love . . .

Several times, it seemed to me that my domestics were trying to tear me away from Eva's room; I struggled; I clung to her bed, to her body . . .

I was in love; yes, I was in love . . .

When, on the morning of the third day, the nascent dawn let its first light filter into the room. I looked, and saw this:

Eva, still motionless; her eyes were vitreous; her swollen face had livid tones, and the open mouth designed a frightful rictus . . .

Then, uttering a scream of fear, I fainted.

II

June 185*

For seven days they thought that I was in danger of death; for seven days my mother, having hastened to my bedside, kept anxious vigil, and the physicians made dubious gestures.

And for seven days, my Eva, you remained with me constantly; for seven days, I spoke to you, I heard you. Enlaced together, we traversed space! Oh, the strange sensation of coolness when you placed your cold hand on my burning brow! What sensual pleasure throughout my being when you placed your lips on mine. My Eva!

But on the eighth day, you didn't return, and when I opened my eyes and looked around in the morning, I heard a voice saying: "He's saved" and I perceived my mother, who was smiling through her tears.

Now they affirm that I am cured; my mother is no longer weeping; the physician has returned to Paris, and when he left, he said: "I no longer have any fear for his reason."

My reason!

Yesterday, beloved, for the first time in a long time, your name emerged from my mouth. I took my mother's hand, and, interrogating her with my gaze, I only said a single word: "Eva?"

My mother went very pale, got up and left my room without responding. But Vincent, my old servant, has told me everything. Your remains, alas, are far from here. You repose among your family, out there in the little cemetery of Baden, in the region of Auray. So far away, and yet so close! It's there that I must go, beloved . . .

I'm going there . . .

I have seen the narrow Breton cemetery where your remains lie, my Eva, out here on the shores of Morbihan, in the shadow of old oaks. They have not even engraved your name on their tomb. For long hours, embracing your sepulchral stone, I have murmured my oaths of amour to you and lent my ear to listen to yours. But only the distant rumor of the ebb-tide and the great sob of the fir trees tormented by the wind responded to my voice.

Not a word from the beloved!

And yet, this time, again, I haven't wept. Why, then, do my eyes seem to be forever empty of tears?

July 185*

No, I can't tear myself away from this place, in which her body resides and her spirit doubtless ought to haunt. Everywhere it might be granted to me to glimpse the dear soul, I go, pushed by my desire. Oh, if, while passing close to me, she only deigned to brush my face!

Often, a boat transports me to one of the isles of Morbihan, which seem consecrated to eternal mourning, where all the women are clad in black, all weeping for some father, son or husband. There, I sit down on a reef and, silent and motionless, shivering at the slightest sound, I plunge into my hope.

Many times also, I climb the tumulus of Saint Michel, the sepulchral mountain that covers the plain of Carnac with its shadow. At my feet the fantastic menhirs extend and stretch, gray on the yellow heath, which seem to have sprung forth from the earth . . . emblems of life engendered by death. Before my eyes, the moving blue of the ocean extends as far as the immobile azure of the sky; and in the distance, sinking into the mist, the tongue of land fringed by the foam of the waves that is the sinister peninsula of Quiberon.

On fine summer evenings, when the setting sun sets the horizon ablaze and makes the waves catch fire, one sees a pale and dubious glimmer appear in the vapors floating over the sea: the little lighthouse that signals the reefs of Port Aliguen. Its light is tremulous and timid, as if ashamed of showing itself in the radiance of the day's end. Gradually, however, the crimson disk of the sun sinks into the ocean, diminishes and disappears . . . dusk blurs everything, and the shadow, gray and then black, envelops it all. The gleam of the lighthouse seems to increase then; its light grows, and soon illuminates the night.

It is thus, beloved, that as your image darkens in the night of my memory, amour grows in my heart and hope shines there.

Yes, I hope and I have faith. I wanted to know the mysterious religion in which you believed. Now, I know and I have understood. I have understood your words of terror when you said: "What chastisement does the hell of life reserve for us?" And I have understood the cry of joy that emerged from your lips: "Jean, we shall find one another again."

O my Eva, I am waiting.

August 185*

Nothing, still nothing. I'm despairing!

August 185*

Was that you, my Eva? No, I can't believe it.

Yesterday, the boatmen transported me to the narrow islet of Gavr'innis. I was sitting on the summit of the enormous tumulus whose green roof shelters the long-inviolate sleep of the Brenns with jade necklaces. The heat was stifling. In the cloudless azure of the sky, the sun darted rays that dazzled as the sea reflected them. No breath of air traversed space. A lugger, trapped by the calm, was reposing on its anchors, entirely asleep. No human sound reached me; only the great rumor of the currents silvered by foam troubled he frightful silence. I was waiting; and always, still, that same uncontented desire for tears . . .

I felt my head curbing under the weight of the day . . . and suddenly, in my ear, feeble but distinct, the chimes of a bell resounded, ringing in some distant church. But what were they ringing? Sometimes, the bell wept a death-knell, slowly. And sometimes it beat with rapid and urgent strokes, as if for a baptism.

At that moment, seeming to respond to that appeal, a bright cloud rose into the air. Was it a cloud? No, for as it drew closer, I distinguished a human form clearly. It had all the characteristics that doctors in Occult Science have described many a time: the second envelope of the soul, visible but impalpable, immaterial matter . . .

Oh, I wasn't asleep, since I wanted to weep . . .

It wasn't you, Eva. The woman was blonde, like you, she had blue eyes, like you, but her features weren't yours; and yet, on the whiteness of her cheeks, I could perceive very clearly the two roseate patches, the memory of which will never be effaced from my memory. She stood before me, silently, and her harsh gaze, her eyes charged with hatred, chilled me with terror.

Effortfully, my numb tongue stammered a name: "Eva!"

The woman started to laugh—yes, it was the same laughter that I thought I had heard on my beloved's death-bed. She extended her hand toward me—and then it seemed to me that I was suffocating. An unknown force gripped me by the throat and squeezed violently. I wanted to cry out, but in vain, and I fell to the ground.

When I opened my eyes again, I was in the bedroom of my inn at Auray, and a physician was standing at my bedside.

"Your cares are superfluous, my dear doctor; the malady from which I'm suffering is not one of those that human science can cure."

※

October 185*

An appeasement has taken placed in my thoughts. My friend Raoul d'Amance has come to find me and I have allowed myself to be taken away like a child. Now, I have resumed my old life. We all laugh together at my dementia—everyone except my mother. Yes, I was mad, and what is worse, ridiculous . . .

And yet. I was so happy in my madness!

Madeleine

I

That day, 25 June 187*, our dinner at the cabaret of the Moulin Rouge had been very cheerful.

The evening was magnificent. The concert of the Champs-Élysées sent us the confused rumor of its strollers, drowned out at intervals by the splendid sound of brass instruments. At dessert, Raoul d'Amance got up, filled the glass of the joyful Vitray and mine, and then made a solemn gesture.

"Messieurs, I propose a toast. I drink to the forty-five years accomplished today by our friend Jean de Tréan!"

He put down his champagne glass, and, becoming almost serious, he went on: "Forty-five years since this morning, and you're the youngest of the three of us!" He sat down again. "Bah! it's unnecessary that it afflicts you. Forty-five years, you see, Jean, is the fine age, the age when a man is finally able to love."

"Yes," I replied, in a melancholy tone, "doubtless because it's the age when one no longer wants to love."

Vitray put on a slightly piqued expression, and darting a glance at the mirror, said: "You're not speaking for us, I suppose . . . even less for you, tenebrous beau, for whom all the women are crazy! Sell me the secret of our elixir of youth, Jean; you scarcely seem twenty, my dear! Only yesterday, in the foyer of the Bouffes, Violette said, talking about you: 'Tréan is an amour.' Lauzun, what!"[1]

He looked at himself in the mirror again, while humming a popular tune, and added: "My dear Jean, I know a woman who, like so many others, is very smitten with you."

"With me?"

"Yes, with you, my dear, and an ingénue in the theater, as well. Come on, you must have noticed her? When you're in the audience, she only performs for you; when she laughs, it's for you alone that she shows her teeth; when she sings, it's for you alone that she spins out her trills. You can't guess? Léa . . . little Léa de Coucy."

"Who is Léa de Coucy?" I asked, indifferently.

"Oh, my dear, don't show so much distaste. Léa is a very pretty woman, even though, according to Violette, she lacks breasts and puts in fake pads . . . and then, a true artiste, although she drags out the high notes too much and stammers when she talks. First honorable mention at the Conservatoire de Toulouse. And with that, a good family. Her father was a professor at the lycée in Agen—professor of gymnastics. Forgivable! It's agreed, then— I'll introduce you!"

I shook my head and, half-joking and half-serious said: "Pointless."

---

1 Antoine Nompar de Caumont, Duc de Lauzun (1632-1723), was said to exercise a strange fascination over women; he became notorious as the object of an obsession on the part of "La Grande Mademoiselle" (Anne, Duchesse de Montpensier), Louis XIV's cousin.

"Why?" retorted Vitray. "Léa's very nice . . . a girl who would do you honor, and . . ."

"Don't persist," Raoul interrupted, squeezing his arm slightly. "Jean's been smitten with someone else for a long time."

"Bah! He should have said. With whom?"

Raoul took my hand. "Poor fellow! He's in love with a phantom . . . a dead woman."

I sensed myself going pale. Twice I filled my glass to the brim, and twice I emptied it in a single draught. Then, launching a burst of laughter: "How appropriate, Raoul, for my birthday, to remind me that I have been mad . . . fit to be tied." After a slight pause I continued: "Yes, I loved a dead woman, a phantom, as our friend Monsieur d'Amance has just said. But, dead or alive, women are all the same: ingrate, forgetful of their promises, perjurers of their oaths. In twenty-two years, Madame Corpse has not deigned to honor me with a single visit. So, it's agreed; tomorrow you can introduce me to Léa de Courcy."

But Vitray had become grave. "No," he said. "You talk about your dead woman, my dear, with your lips taut and your eyes shiny, as a furious and desperate lover would. Personally, I don't know why, when one has loved a woman, one shouldn't want to see her again . . . even if she's dead . . . especially today, when it's so easy to see the dead again!"

A great silence fell.

"Yes," Vitray continued, "I, who am speaking to you, Messieurs, chatted with a woman a week ago, who has been asleep for more than ten years, far away from here, beyond the sea, in a cemetery in America. Oh, don't laugh like that, Raoul, you irritate me with your skeptical airs. I tell you that it was her. It was her hair, her eyes, her mouth. She repeated a secret known to me alone. I'm still sick with fear."

For the fourth time I emptied my glass, and, replacing it noisily on the table, I cried: "Infamous conjuring tricks!"

Vitray stood up, and said, in a dry tone: "Monsieur de Tréan ought to know that I scarcely allow myself to be tricked. Anyway, go to Passy, and at 25 Rue du Ranelagh, ask to see Doctor Allan."

I made no reply.

In the distance a clock chimed ten.

"Ten o'clock!" exclaimed Raoul. "Let's go to the Circus. It's Saturday, when high society goes. Are you coming, Tréan?"

"No thank you, your dinner and stories have muddled my brain too much. I need to sleep; I'm going home."

We quit the Moulin Rouge and found ourselves in the Avenue d'Antin, already almost deserted.

"Goodnight, Monsieur de Tréan," said Viray. "Above all, no bad dreams!"

And they both drew away in the direction of the Circus.

Left alone on the sidewalk, I headed for the Pont des Invalides, desirous of returning home; but my head was heavy and my stride laborious. I was definitely a little drunk.

An empty cab was just passing. I climbed into it.

"Where is it necessary to take Monsieur?"

Then, in a low voice, as if strangled by emotion, I said: "To Passy, 25 Rue du Ranelagh."

II

It was a house of elegant appearance, an odorous cottage, which laburnum and wisteria coated with their variegated draperies. A small garden planted with rose-bushes and lilacs extended before the façade. The entire abode suggested a reposed, perhaps happy life.

In spite of the advanced nocturnal hour, the gate was open and the windows of the house were brightly lit, scintillating in the shadow. Motionless on the sidewalk of the street, I dared not approach; a sentiment of shame held me back. What would I say to Doctor Allan? How could I explain my visit? I wanted to run after my cab, which was drawing away . . . but no; my feet remained nailed to the ground, and the vehicle disappeared into the night. Oh, how violently my heart was beating! What feverish sounds the blood was making in my ears!

For twenty-two years you have wanted to know, Jean; are you going to know, finally?

At an unsteady pace, I traversed the garden and climbed a perron. Like the gate, the entrance door was open. I went into the vestibule. No one . . .

For the second time, shame seized me, but less forcefully. Not daring to call out, I looked around; everything seemed strange to me.

On the walls of the antechamber, perceived, suspended in large numbers, drawings of human figures in black or blood-red, of a truly fantastic aspect. Whether deliberately or by virtue of the inexperience of the artists, the features, confusedly traced and scarcely visible, seemed to be lost in a diaphanous fog; but more bizarre still were the captions inscribed below the portraits:

> Apparition of 1 January 187*: Pierre (still refuses to submit to expiation)
> Apparition of 2 November 187*: Phryné (will submit to her redemption)

In the midst of those drawings, on the white wall, the following lines stood out in red letters:

> *By virtue of three things humans fall back under the necessity of Abred (the Inferno of Life): the absence of effort toward knowledge; scorn of the good and the practice of evil. Triad XXV.*

While observing, I listened.

The sound of voices reached me from a neighboring room. A man was pronouncing words, interrupted at certain moments by murmurs of approval. At times, too, a plaintive melody interrupted the orator's speech or accompanied it mutedly.

Weary of waiting, and making my decision, I tapped my cane on the floor-tiles and called out. A door-curtain was raised and a black-clad domestic came toward me.

"Doctor Allan?" I asked.

The domestic examined me suspiciously for a few seconds. "Monsieur," he said, "is doubtless one of the new adherents invited this evening?"

I nodded my head slightly.

"Well, hurry up," he said. "The mystery has commenced." And he stood aside to let me pass.

I went in.

In a room of vast dimensions, abut thirty people were sitting in chairs arranged in rows. At the back of the room a rostrum had been set up at which a man was standing, speaking while making solemn gestures. He was a tall, aged man with a strange face. Long white hair fell over his shoulders; a bushy beard framed his face, and dark eyes glinted beneath thick eyebrows. The man was not unknown to me.

Sitting by his side and almost at his feet, I perceived a young woman of about twenty. Oh, that one, yes, I had already encountered on the path of my life. But where? Where had I seen that blonde hair, that thin and pale face, those steel-blue eyes? Where? Her head raised toward the old man, she was contemplating him with an amorous admiration, and seemed to be in ecstasy under the charm of his speech.

A place was free in the last row of chairs; I sat down there.

I looked at the woman.

Almost immediately, she turned her head slowly, apparently looking for someone in the audience, and her eyes met mine . . . but with a visible effort, she closed her eyelids and raised her face again toward the man with the white hair.

One of my neighbors murmured: "An unfortunate mystery. What's wrong with Allan this evening? He isn't as brilliant an orator as usual."

Doctor Allan was evidently troubled. However, with his left hand applied to his heart and the right extended toward the assembly, he continued his speech.

"Yes," he said, "death is only a vain word, a syllable devoid of meaning. All of us here present have already experienced successive incarnations, and the Inferno down here will seize us again until our complete redemption. O Death, you are but a renewal of life; O tomb, you are but a cradle. And I, taking inspiration from Saint Paul, want to issue my challenge to you, as my master Yves Mériadec once did, and cry: 'Sepulcher, where is your victory?'"

The name of Yves Mériadec, suddenly thrown into my memory, caused me to shudder. Instantly, the young woman felt a similar commotion; then, turning her head toward me violently, she riveted her gaze to mine again. Now her eyes were staring at me obstinately. But Allan had interrupted himself abruptly. He tried to resume his improvisation but he could only stammer. Finally, his brow inundated with sweat, he was obliged to sit down.

An orchestra composed of a piano and harps started to play a bizarrely modulated harmony.

"The music of a composer who no longer belongs to our earth," my neighbor said to me, again.

In the meantime, Allan, very pale, was examining the young woman fearfully, but she, insensible to everything, still kept her eyes fixed on mine.

Finally, shaking off the torpor of his thought, Allan got to his feet again, and spoke emphatically to invisible beings: "Innumerable spirits of the dead," he cried, "you who surround us, among whom we walk, whom we respire, in whom we live, listen with benevolence to the prayer of your servant! Let one of you deign, for a moment, to unite yourself with the flesh of this living being and become incarnate in her!"

He designated the blonde-haired young woman.

"But no!" he said, interrupting himself. "Such prodigies have been accomplished many times. I sense that the moment has come to attempt something more. Allow, for a moment, the body of this incarnate, this living being of today, to resume its anterior form! For a long time, I have been trying to realize that impossible dream. But a voice has resounded within me, which has said to me: 'Dare!' I want the blind to see! Yes, I want it." He added, forcefully: "Even if my heart must break! Before being a man, I am a priest!"

On hearing those jerky, incoherent words, the assembly was shaken by a long frisson. But Allan, dominating the rumor with a gesture and abruptly extending his finger toward me, he cried: "Monsieur, you whom no one here knows and who have slipped into the temple like a thief in the night, stand up!"

As if struck by an electric shock, I stood up; the woman also stood up.

"Approach!" the doctor ordered.

I marched toward the stage; but at each of my forward steps, the woman took a step back, and, still looking at me, she went to place herself against the wall.

"Of what did you come here in search?" Allan asked me, harshly.

And I replied: "I came in order to know."

He started to laugh, an angry laughter. "So be it! You shall know!"

Paper and a pencil had been placed on the rostrum in advance.

"Write a name," Allan said to me. "Yes, the name that is lust, that is the torture of your heart."

I traced a single word: "Eva."

"Now," commanded the doctor, addressing the young woman, "it's me that it's necessary to obey. Resume your place!"

And with his finger, he pointed to the armchair.

The woman did not budge, still looking at me.

"Well, so be it, Monsieur," said Allan. "You're the stronger—order! You doubtless don't know it, but God has made you a redoubtable medium."

Then, at the mute injunction of my thought, the woman marched toward me. For a moment, she beat the air with her arms, as if she wanted to drive me away, but, her strength exhausted, she sat down heavily in the armchair.

I placed the piece of paper on which Eva's name was written on the woman's breast, and I waited, quaking.

Immediately, an amazing phenomenon was produced. A livid pallor invaded her face; her features contracted and her cheeks, hollowing out, traced two profound pleats around her mouth; an oppressed respiration emerged from her parted lips, succeeded by a cough—the cough with the bloody mucus that precedes death. Finally, the woman uttered a great sigh, and her head fell backwards.

"She is dead!" cried Doctor Allan. "Her heart has ceased beating. Is there a physician here who can certify the fact?"

A member of the audience climbed on to the stage, examined the subject, and declared that the heart had, in fact, ceased beating.

Soon, however, it seemed to me that life entered into the cadaver again. The cheeks colored slightly; a respiration, weak at first, and then regular, lifted the dead woman's bosom; the dead woman came back to life. And then—was it a hallucination of my senses?—oh, then . . . yes, I saw it: her face was transfigured!

Suddenly, I recognized in the pale face the same pink sign on which I had placed my lips twenty-two years before. Eva! Eva herself was before me!

I fell to my knees.

But the dead woman straightened up slowly; she extended her arms toward me, and gently ran her fingers over my forehead, over my eyes and over my mouth.

A very faint voice murmured in my ear: "Jean, it's me . . . it's the beloved."

I uttered a cry of terror and stood up. Allan placed his hand on my shoulder, and said, in a dry tone: "Are you satisfied, Monsieur de Tréan?"

And I, my eyes rendered haggard by fear, stammered: "Marcus!"

III

Oh, what a night, frightful and delectable, full of voluptuous terrors . . .

Eva, finally rediscovered!

IV

The following morning, at ten o'clock, I rang Doctor Allan's doorbell. I was introduced immediately.

Marcus was alone in his study, surrounded by books, working. When I entered, he stood up and bowed slightly, but did not offer me his hand.

"Monsieur de Tréan," he said, "I expected your visit; you had to come."

I took a chair and sat down.

"Do you know, Monsieur," Marcus continued, "that you are a medium endowed with a formidable power? Yes, formidable. What brought you here, good or evil?"

I did not reply.

"Good, doubtless," he continued, after a brief silence. "Your intervention in our mysteries has already produced useful results. Several of yesterday's incredulous are believers today, and henceforward."

He then started speaking to me about a small "Spiritualist" church of which he was one of the priests. Fifteen years before, he had devoted himself entirely to his apostolate; he had quit the name of Marcus in order to take that of Allan, in honor of one of the prophets of the good news, Allan Kardec. Oh, they had suffered a great deal, masters and disciples, ministers and adherents. In Spain, the Catholic clergy had burned their books in public squares; in France the tribunals had thrown several of their pastors in prison. Every day, abominable mockery was heaped upon them; people sought to kill them with ridicule. And yet, their church was growing in strength. Allan estimated at several hundred thousand the followers distributed in Europe; they were even more numerous in America. Eminent men in letters or the sciences adhered to the doctrine: poets, novelists, playwrights, historians, philosophers, astronomers and mathematicians! But it was above all among the disinherited by fortune that the faithful were recruited.

"What other religion," Marcus exclaimed, enthusiastically, "can give a logical and yet consoling explanation of poverty and hunger? Christianity is impotent henceforth to moralize the masses, and the masses are abandoning it. O Nazarene, how did you dare to say: 'There will always be poor people among us'?"

While he was declaiming his sonorous phrases, I listened with a distracted ear. Time was passing. What, was *she* not going to come?"

The door opened. Shivering, I stood up. It was *her*.

She stopped, as if frightened by the sight of me, closed her eyes, placed her hand swiftly against her heart, and turned her head away.

"Oh, that man!" she stammered.

Marcus had approached, and said, designating me: "Madeleine, Monsieur de Tréan."

She seized his hands and bore them passionately to her lips, murmured a few words in a very low voice, and then ran outside.

"Do you know, Monsieur," said Marcus, when we were alone, "what my wife just said to me?"

His wife! *Her*... married! *Her*... Marcus's wife!

"Madeleine said to me: 'Send that man away; he is bringing misfortune here.'"

I remained motionless, stupefied, and faint. Finally, mastering my emotion, I dragged myself to the door.

"I shall never come back here," I said, as I left.

And as I closed the gate of the house, Marcus, who had accompanied me that far, exclaimed, dolorously: "So it was for Evil, then!"

V

1 July 187*

Why, then, had the physician affirmed, twenty-two years ago: "I'll answer for his reason"? My reason! It seems to me, alas, that it foundered a long time ago. And now, the poor madman is turning into a credulous simpleton. What a farce! What a master charlatan that Marcus is! Great pontiff Allan, and you, Madame Madeleine, his worthy spouse, look elsewhere than in the house of a Tréan for your dupes!

But Eva? I sensed myself gripped with shame, as well as self-pity, and the sensate lines of the ancient poet returned to my memory:

> *Love a shadow as a shadow, and of extinct ashes*
> *Extinguish the memory.*

This morning, Vitray erupted into my bedroom.

"Well, Jean, what's become of you? It's two weeks since any-one has seen you, my dear. The entire club is in mourning. Are you ill? How pale you are! Fifteen years more on your head in a fortnight! By the way, have you been to visit the miracle doctor we talked about the other evening?"

I shrugged my shoulders.

"No?" he continued. "Skeptic! Personally, I have a more cheer-ful excursion to propose to you. After dinner, I'll take you to the Bouffes-Parisiens. Young Léa de Courcy is making her debut, and believe me, it's a big event, as the members of the orchestra say. You have to come. The girl is absolutely mad about you; you'd be ashamed of causing chagrin to her little heart. You'll see what a pretty muzzle she has when she's throwing her enticements into the stalls! An adorable foxy face! And the comic! How they laugh in the hall when he looks the ingénue up and down and cries: "That's immense!" Don't protest; the box is booked. Even the sage Raoul is in the party. Above all, don't forget the tea-rose in your buttonhole—your lady's colors! Until this evening, dear chap—I'll come and pick you up."

And Vitray went out, repeating: "Immense!"

Same day

In truth, what do they have in their hearts, my friends? Personally, I can't live like them . . . no, I can't do it.

I want to flee France; I want to extend the distance between my memories and me. Out there, far away, I'll doubtless find a corner of the vast world that will render me repose, forgetfulness of myself.

I'll leave tomorrow.

VI

Naples

I have traversed peoples; cities have passed before my eyes. Always myself, alas! Italy, the land where nature lavishes such charming smiles on people, no ray of your sunlight has been able to descend into my heart.

Further away, further away!

＊

Jerusalem

Jerusalem! O Jesus of Nazareth, you who, you who accord, my mother told me, the tear that purifies, the blessed tear, I have bowed my head over your sepulcher. Why, impotent God, have you not given me tears?

Further away, even further!

＊

Calcutta

Finally, calm will enter my spirit! I have set foot on the old soil of India. This strange world pleases the monstrosities of my thought, and in this ossuary of so many civilizations, in this land of the dead, I hope to die myself.

＊

What have I just learned? Among the letters that were waiting for me in Calcutta I have found one from my friend Vitray. He relates thousands of foolish trivia, but this is what I read:

The séances in the Rue du Ranelagh have ceased. It
appears that Madeleine Allan is very ill.

Ill . . . Madeleine? Well, what does it matter to me?

❋

A ship is leaving tomorrow for Marseille; I shall embark in an hour.

Oh, yes, I want to see her again! I shall see her again . . .

❋

May 188*

Ah! I've seen her again!

VII

May 188*

Yes, I've seen her again. What irresistible power, then, has driven me toward the detested house, and what is that Madeleine making of me . . . Madeleine Allan?

The night was well advanced when I arrived on the Rue du Ranelagh, already in May, still warm, brightly illuminated by the moon. In that remote corner of Paris, all was solitude.

The Rue du Ranelagh, half-built, is bordered by empty plots enclosed by wooden fences. Opposite Allan's house I slipped through a gap in one of those fences. I found myself in an area full of long grass, with a few trees here and there. An old cedar, the debris of a park that had been parceled up, spread its roots over that abandoned garden. I went to lurk in its great shade, and then watched, with my eyes fixed on the house.

Why that absurd escapade, poor Jean? Why that self-degradation?

Everything in Allan's dwelling seemed to be asleep; only one window on the first floor allowed a faint light to pass through.

Ardently, I concentrated my sight and thought upon it.

Time went by. Three o'clock chimed on the distant clock of the church of Passy.

Suddenly, the window opened quietly and Madeleine appeared, clad in white, her hair scattered over her shoulders. I uttered a small cry and, emerging from the shadow that enveloped me, I contemplated her passionately.

She turned her head toward me, undoubtedly perceived me, smiled her same distraught smile and fixed her eyes on mine.

For a long time, we looked at one another thus in the silence of the night, by the light of the stars. And when dawn spread its nascent light over the horizon, Madeleine made an effort to extract herself from her ecstasy. She closed the window again and disappeared.

Amour, rapture of my soul, intoxication of my senses; amour, again you have come to invade my entire being!

VIII

June 188*

For a month, the two of us have been plunged thus into the great ecstasy of grand amour, making our eyes talk and exchanging the words of our hearts from afar. I'm happy! O voluptuousness of suffering, bitter enjoyment of unslaked desires!

Madeleine . . . Eva.

IX

Everything has been accomplished in accordance with Eva's solemn promise; we are bound to one another forever. An immense joy has entered into me, and yet I am afraid.

Yesterday, I slipped away to our habitual rendezvous. The night was hot, strewn with stars, and enervating and voluptuous scents rose from the Bois.

My eyes fixed on the window, I waited, but the window remained closed.

The hours fled, and day was about to break. A poignant anxiety took possession of me, more dolorous with every passing moment, increasing my ardor to see her.

Oh, Madeleine . . . !

And at that imperious appeal of my thought, the door of the house opened, and I saw her, all white, emerging from the shadow . . .

She was standing upright on the threshold of her dwelling, motionless.

Beloved! Oh, Beloved . . . !

Then, as on the night of our first meeting, she made a desperate gesture; then, coming down the steps of the perron slowly, she slowly traversed the garden, opened the gate and advanced into the street . . .

Having reached the wooden fence she hesitated again, turned, and seemed to want to flee . . .

Finally, she came into the enclosure.

I launched myself toward her.

"You!"

Madeleine extended her arms in order to drive me away, and in a muted voice she said: "What do you want with me, Monsieur? Here I am."

I united her hands in mine, drew her toward me violently, and in a passionate enlacement, clasped her to my breast. She threw her head back and closed her eyes.

"No . . . no!" she stammered. "Have pity . . . !"

I brought her face back close to mine by force, and my lips posed on hers . . .

For a long time we remained pressed against one another thus, and for a long time I felt the shivering of her body and the bite of her kisses.

Suddenly, she snatched herself away from my grip. Allan had surged forth before us.

Madeleine fell to her knees, bewildered.

"Kill me, Monsieur; I'm nothing but a wretch. It's me, of my own accord, who delivered myself to this man! And yet," she continued, with a sob, "I swear on my eternal honor that I love you, my master! My lord, I love you! I love you, my husband!"

Allan lifted her up.

"I don't have the right to punish you," he said, "poor debilitated soul, who has twice failed your redemption. But let your destiny be accomplished, and since you have returned down here in order to expiate, expiate!"

Without addressing a single word to me, he took Madeleine back into his house.

I wandered like an insensate all day long.

In the evening, when I went home, my valet de chambre said: "Monsieur, a lady has been here for several hours, who desires to speak to you."

It was Madeleine. When she saw me enter, she stood up.

"Will Monsieur de Tréan deign to give shelter henceforth to an adulterous woman?"

Intoxicated by happiness, I put my arm around her waist and drew her gently towards my bedroom. Then, as we were about to go into it, she uttered a savage laugh, and darting a glance at me full of hatred, she said:

"Wretch!"

Rediviva

2 November 188*

The gate of the château grated as it swung on its hinges and the vehicle penetrated into the courtyard.

At that sound, Madeleine, sitting next to me, shook off the torpor of her thoughts for a moment.

"Where are we?" she asked.

"At the Château de Vauvilliers," I replied.

I felt her tremble in every limb, and silence fell between us again. I was terribly emotional; what was soon about to happen was so grave!

No, certainly, such a torture could not go on any longer. For six months, I had been united, not with a living woman, but with a dead one. The menacing words that Marcus had hurled at me twenty-two years before had been accomplished in all their horror; Madeleine's hatred increased every day. The first delirium of her senses had soon calmed, but at present she abandoned herself to it, icy and impassive, with the sickening resignation of a young woman prostituting herself. Shutting herself away for entire days in a grim mutism, sometimes she wept. Sometimes she allowed her gaze to wander in space, bewildered, as if she had become idiotic.

"So you hate me fervently, then, Madeleine?" I asked her one day.

"Yes," she replied, "I hate you, you who have abused the weakness of a miserable invalid in order to steal from her everything that she loved."

Another time, seeing her weeping, I asked: "Are you suffering, Madeleine?"

"I'm thinking about him."

"Would you like us both to go to implore his forgiveness?"

"No. He'd forgive me, but I don't forgive myself. In any case, am I not condemned to expiate?" She added in a low voice, punctuated by a sob: "Oh, if only I could die!"

To die! And in a passionate embrace, taking possession of me with her hands: "And me, then!"

Yes, but it was necessary to be sure. What if I were the victim of an illusion? What is Madeleine were not my Eva? If . . . well, I was about to convince myself. Had not Marcus revealed it to me? I was a redoubtable medium.

Vincent, the old servant to whom the guard of the château had been confided for a long time, was on the landing, holding a candle. I helped Madeleine down from the carriage and we climbed the stairs. Having arrived on the first floor, I opened a door and, seizing Madeleine's arm, I went into a room: the room where Eva had died.

"Stay awake tonight," I said to my domestic. "I'll doubtless have need of you."

He bowed and went out.

My orders had been carried out scrupulously. Nothing had been changed in that room for twenty-two years. Extended over the wall there was still the faded antique verdure, the gigantic swans floating between frail trees with yellowed foliage. Two candles were burning on the mantelpiece in fleur-de-lysed brass candlesticks. The old Boule pendulum clock told time with its monotonous tick-tock. At the back of the room stood a large canopied bed with its helical columns and its tapestry curtains; near the bed, finally, on a table, were spread the same books that the dying Eva's fingers had riffled through.

Madeleine paraded a haggard gaze over those objects, and for the second time, a frisson of fear agitated her.

Taking her hands, I constrained her to sit down in an armchair, and, in a voice in which all the passion of my heart vibrated, I said: "Madeleine, it's necessary that you love me."

She sniggered dryly. "I'm your slave, your thing," she replied. "I'll try to obey."

She tried to pull her hands away; I retained them forcibly between mine, and kneeling down before her, I said: "Madeleine, I love you; I want you to love me."

She raised her forehead and replied: "You horrify me. You . . ."

She could not say any more, and the insult commenced stopped dead on her lips. Her eyes wide open and her pupils dilated, Madeleine looked at me, but could not speak. The power of magnetism that I had once excised so violently on the woman had returned.

Still holding her hands, I stood up, and with an effort of will, I nailed her to her armchair. She attempted to resist, and struggled; it was in vain. Soon, a profound sigh was exhaled from her breast, and her head fell back.

She was now under my absolute domination.

I carried her away in my arms and deposited her on the bed. Then, sitting down at her bedside, I contemplated her for a long time.

Yes, I loved her, that woman who had nothing for me but detestation and scorn. With what passion I observed her large eyes, the color of steel, her pale face with ivory tints, her scattered blonde hair, and there . . . there, over her cheekbones, the two roseate patches!

And as I buried myself in my contemplation, a distant memory obsessed me. Where had I seen Madeleine before? Through what space, in what world, had we encountered one another?

Suddenly, enlightenment dawned in my mind. *Yes out there on the islet of Gavr'innis, when my head was bowed under the burden of my despair, that menacing apparition, it was you! You . . . ? No, but Eva, since I was evoking her at that very instant! You were, therefore, the new form of her reincarnation. Marcus, in the Mystery of the Rue du Ranelagh, was not mistaken; I was not the victim of an illusion . . . !*

Come on, come on, for the last time, it was necessary to convince myself again . . . and then to act!

I approached my lips so close to hers that our respirations were confounded. Then, in a supreme effort, combining all my desire and all my effort, I commanded:

"Eva, become once again the woman who loves me. I wish it!"

Immediately, the terrible phenomenon that I had witnessed before was produced. The woman's respiration became halting; a rattle grated in her throat; her pulse weakened and stopped; her heart ceased beating.

"Eva . . . ! Eva . . . !" I repeated, in a voice that filled the silence of the room.

And slowly, sitting up at my appeal, Eva herself held out her arms to me. She extended her hands toward my face, and gently ran them over my forehead, over my eyes and over my lips.

"Jean, it's me . . ."

Oh, Beloved . . . ! Finally . . . ! Yes, yes, my Eva, isn't that enough proofs . . . enough tortures . . . enough expiations? Let your final words be accomplished: let us abandon this earth in order to love one another forever in the eternity of worlds!

With both hands I seized the woman's neck and squeezed it for a long time, like a vice. The features of her face convulsed; her eyes looked at me, terribly. Her mouth seems to be laughing.

I squeezed harder. A drop of blood fell and stained the pillow.

Finally, I parted my fingers and released her head; the head collapsed, inert.

The woman was dead.

I precipitated myself toward a revolver hanging in a panoply. I loaded it . . . and then I threw it to the ground. No, that was not the way I had to undergo my punishment.

Then I opened both battens of the door, and with repeated cries, I summoned my domestic. He arrived, fearfully.

"Go," I said to him, "run to Vauvilliers, wake up the men of law. Tell them to hurry. This woman has expiated. It's my turn now."

*

The notes of this journal were given to me last year, after the death of my poor relative, Jean de Tréan, who hanged himself one night in his cell at the lunatic asylum at C***. Three months before, he had passed before the assizes, but the jury, in spite of repeated confessions and a strange desire on the part of the accused to be condemned, acquitted him on the grounds of insanity.

THE BELOVED

All those of our small literary world knew René Jaucourt, a spirit refined to the degree of quintessence, a dreamer to the extent of mysticism. His unexpected death caused some surprise, and even some chagrin in the hearts of the most indifferent, but the fatal and common shroud of forgetfulness is already beginning to weigh upon his memory.

René Jaucourt has left a few volumes of personal memoirs that he destined for print. His testamentary executors, however, have not yet wanted to publish them, thinking that such a book might denounce the aberration of a mental illness. That is not our opinion, and from the manuscript of that posthumous author we have extracted the very curious love story that you are about to read; the public will hear the case and decide. "A hallucinate," a few clever individuals will say, "an insensate and delirious soul." What does it matter? For us, the vision of the occult is not a deviation of human reason; and then, if wisdom, as Leibniz says, is only the science of happiness, René Jaucourt, the pretended madman who was able to die happy, was a veritable sage.

I

. . . .
That evening, hoping finally to grasp the inspiration that was fleeing me, I set to work ardently. In any case, it was raining torrentially: an April downpour flagellating Paris, rattling and

splashing. "No, I won't be going out"—and I dismissed my domestic. Nine o'clock had just chimed at the Chapelle Saint-François de Sales; under the spring rain, the Avenue de Villiers extended silently, and the slumber of the peaceful quarter was already commencing. Lighting a cigarette, I stretched myself out in an armchair and was soon absorbed in mid-dream,

I was preparing a "theurgical tale," a strange fantasy, the apparent extravagance of which would doubtless alarm the indolence of the illiterate, but the dream of which enabled me to forget the excessively cruel banalities of life. I have always disdained the favor of the vulgar, and once again, I did not want to amuse them. The initial idea for my story, borrowed from the mystical doctrines of neoplatonism, had captivated my imagination immediately, bearing it away toward the fascinating terrors of the beyond.

I supposed two human creatures who had loved one another adulterously in the course of their terrestrial pilgrimage. After death, condemned by the clement justice of the divine Being to be subjected to the redemption of their fault, the man and the woman had to traverse a second incarnation. But the two souls encountered one another again on earth; they loved one another again. What would ensue from that second passionate impact? There my concept was still obscure, enveloped by fog and doubt; I could not see. For two months my commenced story had been interrupted, and in spite of obstinate efforts, an unhealthy torpor seemed to be numbing my thoughts.

I did not believe, moreover, in the religion of the occult that is beginning to seduce so many minds and impassion so many hearts nowadays with a renewal of faith. Very curious about the unknown, I had published several fantastic tales, but without conviction, by virtue of a simple liking for the strange. Skeptical and rational, I was not sincere with myself. What caprice, therefore, had impelled me to choose such a bizarre literary subject, a story commenced six months before, interrupted, taken up again, which I did not know and could not finish?

An hour went by. Outside, the April squalls were still moaning, and the rain lashing my study window with rapid thrusts. Extended in my armchair, my eyes closed and my hands joined, I evoked my two phantoms, striving to design their contours, to knead their flesh and breathe life into them. As on the previous day, however, my creation was difficult and my imagination agitated fruitlessly. Nothing! I could not find anything . . .

Suddenly, I shuddered: a lamentable sob had just traversed the silence of my solitude. One might have thought it a groan, or rather a cry for help, uttered by the voice of a woman, brief, shrill and heart-rending. The plaint vibrated, and then she fell silent.

Slightly surprised, I had sat up straight, and now I paraded my gaze around me . . .

No further sound: doubtless an illusion! I was certainly alone in the room; my books surrounded me, displaying their gleaming bindings; on my mantelpiece, a bronze Buddha was meditating, inhaling the endless quietude of Nirvana, and in front of me, my father's portrait was gazing at me sadly, as ever. Finally, however, my eyes turned toward one of the corners of the room and I soon experienced a sort of fascination. Over there, a piano was open, and in the light of my lamp the ivory of its keys was shining, glinting attractively.

"Ah!" I exclaimed, laughing. "So it's you who are weeping like that. One of your strings must have broken—a simple effect of the storm."

Getting up, I went to sit at the keyboard, and my fingers ran through the octaves rapidly. No, nothing was broken; every note resonated clearly and accurately . . .

How long did I remain there, threading notes, detailing arpeggios? Only a few seconds; but suddenly, I was gripped by an inexpressible anguish, and for no reason, my eyes swelled with tears. With a mechanical movement, my fingers had just played a naïve melody, and I recalled a memory that I had thought effaced forever.

It was an old ballad from a light opera, one of those sentimental ariettas in the fashion of the reign of Louis XVI, from *Nina, ou La Folle par amour.*[1] The tune is simple, soft, full of melancholy, and no one is unaware of the reverie that it once imported to the hearts of "sensitive women," the amiable readers of a Parny or a Bertin.[2] I had never heard Dalayrac's ballad at the theater, or even at a concert, and yet it came back to me incessantly; I sang it, I hummed it, experiencing the mist inexplicable emotion in its repetition.

When the beloved returns
To his languishing friend
Spring will be reborn.
Plants will flower again . . .

I had even had a pleasant, stupidly ridiculous adventure in my youth, which had caused momentary alarm for my reason.

On one snowy evening in December, Christmas Eve, I had gone into the church of Saint-Sulpice. Why? I don't know; but at night, I love to plunge into the holy darkness that envelops infinity then and absorb myself in all the harmonies of divine silence. The solitary nave extended, still odorous with the perfume of incense, its meditative darkness scarcely pricked by the ruddy gleam of widely-spaced lamps.

A sound of voices soon rose up, very faint, departing from the crypts of the church; down below, in the catechism chapel,

---

1 *Nina, ou La Folle par amour* is a one-act opera-comique by Nicolas Dalayrac, with a libretto by Benoît-Joseph Marsollier ds Vivetières, based on a short story by Baculard d'Arnaud; it was first performed in May 1786, with Louise Dugazon in the title role. It was a great success and was revived several times, remaining in the company's repertoire until the middle of the nineteenth century. Hector Berlioz referred to the aria cited as his first musical experience, after hearing an adaptation of it sung during his first communion—an anecdote echoed in the present story.
2 The references are to the Romantic poet Évariste de Parny (1753-1814) and the journalist Louis-François Bertin (1766-1841).

little girls were repeating a canticle. I could not make out the words, but I knew the song that they were singing very well: the aria from *Nina*, the ballad of the beloved. Gently, the chant calmed, caressed and soothed my being, like the distant concerts in the mildness of a dream that make the sleeper smile and weep. And a woman's voice came toward me, striking and magnificent, seemed to utter a desperate appeal:

> *. . . But I look, alas, alas!*
> *The beloved does not return!*

Who, then, was crying out in sobs toward all amour, all well-being, toward the ideal? I stopped, bewildered, collapsed on a chair, and listened for a long, long time . . .

Finally, the voice fell silent. At that moment, an old priest came out of the sacristy. I ran to meet him.

"Who is the great artiste who was audible just now?"

He looked at me, surprised. "What do you mean, Monsieur?"

"Yes, yes, down there, in the crypt of the church, that sonorous and suppliant voice?"

The priest examined me, without response, and then shrugged his shoulders and moved away. Had he taken me for a madman, then?

And many years had gone by since then . . . so rapidly . . . taking away from my mind the remembrance of that Christmas vigil, the harmonious church and the unknown voice that spread out in sobs. How many times, however, had I murmured that passionate prayer myself, addressing it not to the Creator, alas, but to the creature, and with all my prayers, appealing to the beloved!

But life had been inclement to me; pursuing grand amour on earth, I had only encountered banal adventures or temporary liaisons—simple intrigues born of a smile that died without a tear. Past forty now, I felt very old, partaking of the ash and the dust, and in the despair of my heart, entirely devoted henceforth to my literary métier, I only wanted to be smitten with phantoms, children of my own fantasy . . .

Why, then, had my eyes rediscovered tears so abruptly, and what tenacious folly was making me weep for myself again?

Utterly enervated, I quit my piano. Let's get to work! Forget others and self-absorption! This time, old or not, I was determined to force inspiration. In order to facilitate meditation, I lowered my lamp, and, lighting another cigarette, I extended myself on a divan . . .

Outside, the storm was now calling a truce; the rain had stopped, and, in a sky in torment, the moon was distributing its white light at intervals. Abruptly, one of its rays fell into my cabinet and went to spread out on the wall at the other side of the semi-obscure room. Immediately, in the penumbra, an object began to shine fantastically.

With a curious eye, I followed the play of that light, and even strove to describe it. It was difficult to render the color of that lugubrious light in words . . . Pallid? Livid? Blue-tinted? Phosphorescent? Milky? No . . . wretched epithets, and so banal. Oh, why, then, was that thing over there gleaming, glittering, appealing to me thus? Craning my neck, I looked and I recognized a small engraving framed under glass, a joyous colored image of the eighteenth century. It had only taken its place in my collection a few days before. I had noticed it one morning in the window-display of a merchant on the Quai Voltaire, and suddenly, drawn into the shop, I had bought it . . . it was so amusing to behold!

The artist, the author of the design—*Debucourt sculp. 1787*—had wanted to represent one of the amusing scenes of our Parisian life.[1] His engraving showed us a nocturnal fête in a garden, illuminated by the light of lanterns and fireworks. In the

---

1 The reference (slightly misrendered in the original) is to the painter and engraver Philibert-Louis Debucourt (1755-1832), who produced several images of the Ranelagh Gardens and the dandies who frequented them.

distance, on a stage, musicians were giving a concert in the open air; some Dugazon of the lower orders was singing an arietta, perhaps the adorable ballad from *Nina*. In the foreground of the engraving, a young woman, giving her arm to her excessively old husband, was walking through the fête, and behind them a primped-up coxcomb was dogging their footsteps.

The lady, quite marvelous, was wearing aristocratic costume: an elongated bodice, bouffant skirts beneath double flaps, a high "Léonard" hairstyle and a vast "Pamela" hat. An Englishwoman, surely, that Eucharis—I was certain of it—a sensitive soul, a compatriot of Clementine and Clarissa Harlowe. A bouquet of white florets was pinned to the beauty's belt. And while chatting with her spouse, the darling was extending her hand behind her back, and, leaning toward her, the Lovelace, her sweetheart, was depositing a lover's kiss upon it. The only explanation of the libertine scene was the caption at the bottom of the engraving: *Le Ranelagh de Passy*.

I have always delighted in old images; they are very suggestive to me, and sometimes, while studying them, I think that I am reliving the past. That one, above all, amused me madly. Why? The subject was rather vulgar, but the execution seemed so charming. Every morning I spent long moments contemplating it, and that evening, again, it attracted me . . . irresistibly. I got up and, turning up my lamp, I headed toward it.

Suddenly, my attention was deflected; my eyes had just perceived another object fallen on the carpet directly beneath the fascinating engraving: a large card, goffered and glossy, at which I looked immediately. It too, like the ivory of my piano and the gilded frame of my engraving, was shiny, glittering attractively . . . assuredly a bizarre play of the light, and perhaps an unhealthy cerebral overstimulation. I bent down and picked it up. Oh, my God, an invitation for that very evening to a musical recital hosted by Doctor Legaux! Martial Legaux, my dear friend, a former comrade! And I had forgotten it!

"Well, no, I won't work tonight. To the devil with my phantoms!"

I looked at my watch: only eleven o'clock; I still had time. I got dressed in haste, therefore, and I went out.

II

Doctor Legaux lived in a sumptuous apartment, as vast as a house, on the Boulevard Saint-Germain. During the winter season, dear Martial hosted several fêtes there, which he qualified modestly as "intimate," but at which all Parisian high society gathered. There was singing, plays were performed, and some long-haired poet declaimed his verses.

Four or five years older than me, Legaux had been a comrade at college and our paths through life had crossed many times since; but while I had lingered on the route, a seeker of the ideal, a poor fool pursuing the chimera with a heavy tread, that sage had made progress on his path; he had now attained the goal of his human ambition: an officer of the Légion d'honneur, a member of the Academie de Médicine and a candidate for the Institut. In the meantime, an amiable companion and a fashionable specialist, having acquired renown and fortune, Legaux was greatly admired by his male clients and pampered by his female ones, one of the fortunate of the earth!

In spite of his protective postures, I liked him well enough, knowing myself to be superior. Nevertheless, I rarely abused his invitations; the pretentious banality of my salon fatigued me, and I had not been to visit him that winter. So, as my carriage carried me toward the Boulevard Saint-Germain, I interrogated myself curiously without being able to respond: "What whim is impelling you to run toward ennui this evening? What the devil are you going to do in that galley?"

To go home would decidedly have been wiser. Having reached the Pont de la Concorde, I ordered the coachman to turn back—

but no! Almost immediately, I shouted to him to resume his route. The galley was definitely attracting me.

Midnight had already chimed when I went into Martial Legaux's dwelling. The musical fête had been agitating for a long time, noisily; its "intimacy" was overflowing and, more fortunate than the house of Socrates, the dear doctor's apartment was crammed with friends. In the antechambers and the buzzing dining room, an entire mob of messieurs were chatting and showing off—writers, musicians and painters, magistrates and politicians, a few brokers from the Bourse and very few physicians—with venomous malevolence or solemn stupidity. I knew almost all of them, and exchanged salutes or handshakes in passing.

Martial Legaux was not among them, so I headed for the drawing room. On the threshold, however, I was obliged to stop; the door was barred to me by a compact hedge of broad backs. Women had taken possession of the drawing room, transformed into a concert hall, and the men, expelled, were standing outside like storks. It was impossible to penetrate. Already bored and cursing myself again, I turned back.

At that moment, I heard myself called. "Monsieur Jaucourt! Dear and illustrious master!"

It was another "master" who was addressing me thus, but a master of the magistracy, a petty advocate, a young gentleman of the robe. I knew him—and how!—for having employed him, alas, in a tedious lawsuit; he had hired out his eloquence to me at a high price, had lost my case, and had assassinated me ever since with interested smiles and trivial flattery; he believed himself to be a poet, and dared to write verses. Whenever we met he subjected me to the latest products of his muse, and thus inflicted the cruelest of tortures on me. I did not tax him with any of my consultations, and the wretch abused me! He took me by the arm in a familiar manner.

"How hot it is! It's stifling here. Let's go into the gallery, dear master; we can converse more easily there."

And the individual drew me away, towing me through the crowd.

The gallery in question, a long corridor carpeted with Flemish greenery, was almost deserted for the moment. Resigned to my torture, I let myself fall on to a divan, and my pest sat down beside me.

"I'm annoying you," he said, "perhaps importuning you." Then, without awaiting my response, he went on: "A new poetic venture, but this time, very bold: triolets!"

His broad lawyer's face, framed by russet side-whiskers, designed a rictus that wanted to be a smile. "Yes, triolets, dear master—and amorous triolets!"

Bah! Amorous, that advocate? Implausible! I repressed a sigh, and the torturer set to work. Alas, his triolets were not at all amorous, devoid of lightness and badinage: leaden alexandrines that unfurled and spilled forth, redundant, rambling and repetitive. *Oof!*

Suddenly, I stood up, stupefied.

Back there, someone was singing in the drawing room: muffled by the distance, a woman's voice had just reached me. In the banal murmur of the fête, I could only perceive confused sounds, but that voice vibrated throughout my being, striking and magnificent, similar to the one I had once heard on Christmas Eve in the church of Saint-Sulpice. Similar? Even better: the same! Illusion, surely; a mental disturbance! I sat down again, very emotional, and strove to resume my conversation.

"Very pretty, Monsieur, your triolets. You're a born poet. What a pity that the bar . . ." I stopped. "Oh! But who is that singing, back there? Back there . . . ?"

My advocate lent an ear. "I can't hear anything," he said. "Nothing at all."

I had a moment of impatience. "But yes, Monsieur . . . someone is singing . . . and what passionate, heart-rending tones! Please, let's both be silent."

He looked at me, surprised, bowed stiffly, and went away. Then, closing my eyes and tilting my head back, I listened, motionless. Now the voice reached me more distinctly. I recognized the melody and the words.

When the beloved returns
To his languishing friend . . .

The beloved? Who, then?

I stood up and, with a hasty step, headed toward the drawing room . . . nothing any longer! The concert had just finished; everyone was abandoning the place; the women were forming groups to chatter and the men barring the door had dispersed. Nevertheless, I recognized one of them and interrogated him.

"Can you tell me the name of the diva who has just sung Dalayrac's ballad so well?"

He started to laugh. "A Dalayrac ballad? You're joking: a café-concert refrain; 'I've got the blues' sung by Mademoiselle Nini—you know her, Nini of the Alhambra-Comique . . . eh!" What a suggestive nudge and wink!

The error was amusing; I too began to laugh and went into the drawing room. My friend Legaux was there. Surrounded by bare shoulders, he was being amiable, agitating from one to another, quaking, sniggering and saying insipid things. I advanced to join him . . .

Abruptly, and involuntarily, I was obliged to stop.

It seemed to me that, like a grip of an invisible hand, an unknown force seized my head, and, with a very gentle pressure, turned it slowly, very slowly. Then, I perceived, sitting, or rather huddled, in a corner of the room, a young woman, who was looking at me. Very simply clad in a black silk dress, only having a bouquet of white violets for a corsage, she was wearing an almost severe mourning, without affectation. Quite tall, and slender, with an elegant and delicate figure, she appeared, nevertheless, not to be very pretty. The profile was a trifle strong, and its lines already too pronounced, but the ensemble of the physiognomy had nobility and indicated breeding.

What might the age of the unknown woman be? At first—and I was not mistaken—I supposed her to be thirty-five. A bloodless pallor was spread over her face, and two wrinkles hollowing out their furrows at the corners of her lips denounced some resigned and silent suffering on her part. Of smiles, those lips could only have known the distress. Admirable black hair unfurled its tresses around her head; prominently arched eyebrows stood out against the whiteness of her face, and large blue eyes ringed with bistre brightened the dolorous strangeness of the visage.

And she was looking at me.

I remained still, contemplating her, studying her in detail, gripped—I had no idea why—by an incomprehensible emotion. Where, then, at what turning of the road of my life, had I encountered her before? Yes, I knew her, and yet I had forgotten her name!

Finally extracting myself from that ecstasy of sorts, I went hastily to join Martial Legaux. I bowed to him, and then took him aside.

"Who is that young lady?" I asked him. "In front of us . . . large blue eyes and charming black hair?"

"Madame de Planor."

That baroque name, with a Breton inflexion, told me absolutely nothing; I was hearing it pronounced for the first time.

"A curious physiognomy," I said. "A Parisienne?"

"No, an Irishwoman, but brought up in France: a distinguished mind, a good musician, writes elegant prose, even a few verses, a woman of letters of sorts, but so timid and benevolent!"

I listened, surprised and disappointed. My memory did not recall any of those details. No, I did not know her, that Madame de Planor.

"Is she married?" I asked, already too emotional.

"Yes, to a rather bizarre individual, an illuminate believing in all the stupidities of spiritism and practicing them. He's founded a religious sect and spends a rather large fortune collecting followers: an old madman. But the fellow has a taste for belles-lettres; he appreciates your writings. Madame de Planor also reads your books assiduously; she has mentioned you to me several times. Would you like to be introduced to her . . . ? Yes? Well, let's go over."

Slowly, fraying a path through the groups, we advanced toward the young woman; but my friend was forced to halt continually, obliged to address some word of welcome to one or another of his guests. And during those brief intervals I felt my disturbance increasing; my heart either beat violently or stopped, anguished . . .

Yes, certainly, I had encountered that young woman with the sad smile somewhere; I had seen those large, soft eyes before; I knew all the despair of their long, heart-rending gaze.

She was now tilting her head toward us, watching me approach—still so pale!

Abruptly, she got up, and went to join a man who, standing not far away from her, was examining us intently.

That was a person of odd and fantastic appearance. He must have been about sixty-five. His tall, thin body was inclined, slightly stooped; his entirely bald cranium was shiny under the light of the chandeliers; his sunken black eyes were gleaming under bushy eyebrows, and an extensively graying beard fanned out over the plastron of an embroidered shirt. Had it not been for that Assyrian beard, one might have thought, on seeing him, of one of those grimacing heads that appear to be bursting into laughter in the ossuary of Saint-Pol-de-Léon. Very correctly dressed, he was nevertheless wearing in the buttonhole of his coat—an extravagant joke—a little lotus of sculpted gold, and on the index finger on his left hand an Egyptian scarab was glittering, a turquoise mounted in a ring.

"There's Monsieur de Planor," said Martial Legaux. "Come on . . . you're about to meet a great eccentric."

At that moment, with a fearful gesture, the young woman seized her husband's arm, murmured a few words to him and seemed to want to draw him away from us. But he disengaged himself and came to meet us rapidly.

"Monsieur de Planor," said my friend, "permit me to introduce a dear comrade, Monsieur René Jaucourt, whose name you know and whose writings you have doubtless read."

The man with the Ninevite beard extended his hand to me. I shook it silently, and I felt the Egyptian ring, the turquoise scarab, pressing into my flesh. As for the young woman, she was suspended once again from her husband's arm, and seemed to be trying to draw him away from me.

"Yes, Monsieur Jaucourt," the fantastic individual finally replied, "I know your name, and Madame de Planor and I greatly appreciate your works. Certainly, no one in France has divined the occult better than you and described its fascinating terrors in a broader manner. With a guide like you, one loves to plunge into the unfathomable abyss. One reproach, however! You neglect the philosophy of our doctrines too much and seem to be unaware of its redoubtable morality. Why do you never mention karma?"

Karma? That unusual word was ringing in my ears for the first time. Monsieur de Planor saw my bewilderment, and smiled, slightly ironically, even disdainfully.

"Oho! You have a great deal yet to learn, Monsieur. Madeleine," he went on, turning to the young woman, "invite Monsieur Jaucourt to honor us with his visit; you are better able than anyone to reveal to him all the mystery of second incarnations."

He had expressed himself with a fanatical emphasis, accentuating every word with a gesture, and beneath the blackness of his eyebrows, his little eyes glittered with an interior flame.

"Yes," he continued, "we ought to initiate this curious seeker of the unknown into our doctrines. A mind like his merits our attempting its conquest . . . its glorious conquest!"

Then, slowly, keeping the gaze of her motionless eyes fixed on mine, Madame de Planor extended her hand to me. At the same time she smiled, silently. I seized that hand ardently, and, in accordance with the new custom, inclining toward her, I deposited a kiss upon it. At the contact of my lips, however, Madame de Planor uttered a faint cry. She threw herself backwards and appeared to faint.

I launched myself toward her. "My God! Madame . . . what's wrong?"

She uttered a long, nervous laugh; then, still and always staring at me, but without replying to me, she said to Monsieur de Planor: "For pity's sake, my friend, let's go!"

Also very emotional, he had gone very pale. For a moment, it seemed to me that his eyes darted a defiant threat at me—but the flash was immediately extinguished.

"We'll go," he said to the young woman. And, addressing me again, simultaneously grotesque and solemn, he said: "Monsieur Jaucourt, do you know the pious Angevin legend of your patron saint, the blessed Bishop René? He was a pagan Decurion, the senator of a city that he perverted by his atheism as well as the excesses of his life. The corrupted people followed his example. God then wanted the sinner to die, but to resuscitate him immediately, in order that, a son of death, he would henceforth bear witness to life."

The illuminate paused; then, taking a brightly-colored pamphlet of hieratic aspect from his pocket, he said: "Take it, Monsieur. Dare to read, and above all to comprehend. The Eternal Now is summoning you!"

III

. . . Then, having returned home, and being unable to sleep, I picked up the pamphlet that Monsieur de Planor had given me. It was a booklet of some forty pages, resembling a periodical publication. On the satiny whiteness of its cover a red circle surrounding triangle stood out, and beneath that cabalistic sign was the title of the periodical.

REDEMPTION

The Organ of the Frères-unis de France
Theosophy—Esotericism—Experimental Occultism

Directors: William Allis and Jean de Planor

"O Death, where is thy victory?"

Office and Sanctuary:
Chez Monsieur de Planor, 155 Notre-Dame-des-Champs

On the reverse of the first page the names of the "principal collaborators" were inscribed: bizarre names, extravagant pseudonyms: The Epopt Porphyros; Sâr Eliphas; the Medium Aleph; The Isiac Hierophant Anastasius; the Yogi of Bengal; The Pandect of Djaggernath; Jonas; the *Exitus foras* Lazarus; the Expiator Jean de Planor (I.S.); William Allis . . .

Alone of all the editorial staff, William Allis did not bear any high-flown title. In addition, a marginal note informed the reader of the hidden meaning of the two capital letters I.S. They stood for *incarnation second*. The Expiator Jean de Planor had already traversed the tomb.

The first article of that surprising revue, signed "Jean de Planor," contained a confused dissertation on the mysterious term karma. Written in an apocalyptic style, the overlong literary farrago reproduced, in a leisurely fashion, all the neoplatonist reveries of an Iamblichus or a Porphyry, the Druidic pseudo-doctrines once defended by Jean Reynaud or Henri Martin, and above all the charlatanesque stupidities of the late Allan Kardec and his spiritist colleagues.

I knew them, in any case, those demented theories: the obligation of every human creature to traverse the ordeals of successive lives, to know good and ill fortune, wealth and poverty, domination and humility, the intoxications of amour and its despairs; thus to be, by turns, Lucullus the rich and Lazarus the beggar, Caesar enthroned on the sublimity of the Palatine and the pariah vegetating under the straw, Cleopatra sleeping in Antony's arms and the prostitute shivering in the mud of her sidewalk—for this had to kill that—until the day when, completely purified, the human soul was judged worthy of resuming the course of its sidereal ascent, to rise by degrees toward the just Being and the implacable Clemency, the Ever and the Forever, the Eternal Now . . .

"Hell," proclaimed Monsieur de Planor, "is not, as a crude theology supposes, the exterior darkness from which no one can emerge, the pitiless Gehenna that wounds without amending and would kill even hope. No, and we all know it; it is on earth, it tortures us and destroys us, but it can have pity, for it is ourselves."

One passage, however, of that confused rhapsody, astonished me as much by its strange audacity of thought as its style.

"Karma! When, having escaped its carnal prison at the moment of death, the human soul wants to launch itself toward the light, it is suddenly brought back to the nether regions that it is striving to flee; agitating, but in vain, it cannot surpass the zone of terrestrial attraction. A burden, formidably heavy, weighs upon it irresistibly; that is karma, the burden of its own sins, accumulated in space, which falls upon it and crushes it. Then, the wretched entity finds itself violently cast into the immense zone of shadow that our globe prolongs toward the ether; and there, borne away by the rotation of our planet, it spins, spins relentlessly, until the day when, weary and breathless, it cries toward God and requests to redeem its crimes by means of a second incarnation.

"Karma, therefore, is the burden of actions accomplished by us during our long pilgrimage among humans. If light, it bears us toward absorption in the infinite; if heavy, it casts us down into Hell on earth."

But the most harrowing and the most dangerous of all those follies was attached to an article signed William Allis. I had already noticed that name, placed in an advertisement on the cover of the spiritist revue, without a hieratic title and a grotesque pseudonym. English or American, the man must occupy an important rank in the little French theosophist church, for his prose had been printed in a large font. It was a sort of pastoral letter sent by that individual, who was traveling in India. Like Saint Paul, having "set forth in order to announce the good news," addressing himself to the neophytes of Corinth or Rome, William Allis, "pilgrim of God," wrote to "brothers united by the tomb."

"Never forget, beloved," he said, "that we are not alive, but dead. Reincarnate expiators, for us, all doctrine as well as all morality is summarized in a single word: *Redemption*. Let us therefore dare, phantoms clad in flesh, to strip away that flesh; souls hungry for God, let us no longer have anything of the human. O my dear dead-alive, I implore you, let us be able to die by ourselves."

In spite of that sentimental phraseology, however, the tone of the homily was soon altered; the voice of a high priest made itself heard therein, imperious and fulminating. Allis dogmatized, and promulgated his decrees like a Pope.

"This is what the Eternal Now commands you to do via my mouth, Frères-unis de France:

"No more social poverty! Let the rich man among you distribute his fortune among his brethren, without regrets. A mere steward of God, he has not received the deposit of his gold in order to possess, but to share. If he retains, he steals. Who then, dares say: *this is mine*, since you do not exist yourself?

"No more political despotism! What! You want to reign over humans and have not been able to govern yourself, you whom the weight of your karma has cast you down again upon the earth? O kings who dare to say: *I possess my kingdom*, you are more foolish than the guardian of a necropolis who cries: *I command my tombs!*

"No more terrestrial fatherland! Let the soldier throw away his weapon and tear up his flag. The odor of human slaughter is abominable to the One who has created us brethren by the first cry of birth, and the last gasp of death!

"No more family according to the flesh! Let the lover separate from his mistress and the husband from his wife. What point is there in procreating beings who do not come from you, and who will one day be reborn without you? What a lie, in any case, the word family is! Reincarnate souls, are your children truly more than they are of their anterior parents?"

That formulation of pretended morality went on a lot further, enjoining a complete and lamentable sacrifice of the human personality. The prophet Allis, nevertheless, seemed to renounce momentarily the establishment of his ideal anarchism; in a final chapter of his homily, he prescribed a transitory state: Brothers," he cried, "everything belongs to everyone. Let us therefore dare to put the family in common: the wife, our spouse, and the child, our child. It is, above all, in amour that it is necessary to kill the self."

Letters followed in which a few of the unhinged, adhering to the doctrine, imposed voluntary proofs on themselves: a sort of Vedantic *tapas* exerted in order to hasten "redemption." Here, a man abandoned all his fortune to the community of the Frères-unis; there a father offered it his children; further on, a wife deserted the conjugal house in order to offer herself to the entire sect. In addition, a marginal note informed us that William Allis had just founded a sort of seminary in Ceylon in which brothers and sisters would live henceforth "in a complete and mutual absorption of their souls." It was there, apparently, that the self would be killed.

Finally, the "documentary illustration" did not belie that stupefying revue: a rather bad lithograph reproduced a frightful scene of spiritism. Lying inert on the ground, a man with long hair and a bushy beard appeared to be quaking, prey to all the throes of death. His fists were clenched, his mouth grimacing a rictus, his immeasurably wide eyes convulsed in their orbits. And from all his being a luminous fluid was emerging, a phosphorescent whiteness that, by a slow amalgamation, was progressively forming a body: the body of a woman, smiling and holding a flower in her hand.

The only commentary on that monstrous composition was the text contained in a caption: *The medium Aleph materializing a soul.*

Those emphatic ignominies were displayed at length, filling the theurgical revue with their demoralizing insanities. But while I read that canticle to death, life was already penetrating with a full radiance into my room, and the sun sent me its laughter, its burst of laughter. I closed the pamphlet again and pushed it away in disgust. Throughout the day I did not give it another thought; I devoted myself to my customary occupations; I went to my club; I made a few visits; then I tried to work—but in vain.

In the evening of that same day, there was a première at the Comédie-Française, where all of literate Paris would gather. I dined early, and soon headed for the Rue de Richelieu. The sky was stormy, very heavy, charged with lightning, and the humid warmth caused me a dolorous enervation.

I was early. When I arrived at the theater the principal play had not yet commenced, and in an almost empty hall, they were hastening to raise the curtain. I did not go in. Under the arcades that surrounded the facades, the critics of the dailies, the weeklies and the evening papers were walking in groups, fat and thin, clean-shaven and hirsute, sniggering, pontificating, deflowering the new work, and already drawing one another to malevolence. An author myself, I had never cultivated that vile society; it had too often been cruel to me. I looked at it askance and passed on. I still had plenty of time ahead of me—a long quarter of an hour—before going to cook myself under the gaslight. Traversing the Place du Carrousel, therefore, I went on to the Pont des Saints-Pères . . . and then, on the way, I began to think about my fantastic tale. I went on, hastening my steps, as if I were trying to pursue and track the fugitive idea. At the same time, I thought about Monsieur de Planor, "the expiator." Planor, the man of the "second incarnation." He was repellent to me, that old madman. What a charlatan! Yes, I felt myself in a humor to detest him. Why?

Suddenly, I stopped. A clock had just chimed nine. I looked around: the Rue Notre-Dame-des-Champs! I found myself outside Monsieur de Planor's house: the house where she lived . . . her . . . Madeleine.

IV

It was an elegant detached house in the Louis XV style, with a fronton, pilasters, and scrolled scallops. Constructed in the last century, perhaps to serve as a bijou residence and gallant house, it was now the "sanctuary" where the Frères-unis gathered and where their dementia must agitate. Nothing in that dainty chocolate box, at any rate, could have denounced a church, naos or pagoda, save for a black marble plaque nailed to the wall and engrave in silver letters. *Suffering is redemption*, said the legend. *Ye who want to suffer, enter.*

By the light of a street-lamp, I had been reading and rereading that funereal joke when the door swung open slowly. I heard a little dry laugh and found myself face to face with Monsieur de Planor. I recognized him immediately by his deathly pallor and his skeletal frame, his bushy beard of an archmage and the little lotus flower, the gold of which stood out against the blackness of his garment. He was not alone; in his company another person emerged, who seemed to me to be the medium Aleph—the monsieur who was able to materialize souls. The spiritist lithograph had depicted his grim aspect and bestial physiognomy rather well.

"You!" cried Monsieur de Planor, perceiving me. "Already!" And he started to laugh, again.

His "already" appeared to me to be so impertinent that I did not take the hand he held out to me.

"Monsieur," I said to him, feigning indifference. "I chanced to be passing, and . . ."

He interrupted me. "No, dear master, you were not passing by chance: you have come."

Monsieur de Planor approached me, placed his hand on my shoulder and solemnly indicated the inscription on the black marble to me. "Ye who want to suffer enter! Be welcome, Monsieur René Jaucourt."

There was a brief silence between us. I gazed at that grotesque marionette; was he mocking or did he want to be serious? The insolent smile was no longer parting his lips, but his little dark eyes were gleaming ardently.

"What a pity," he went on. "I would have liked to prepare a brilliant welcome for your visit, but I find myself obliged to go out this evening: an imperious duty. I'm going to the Gare de Lyon, where our brethren are gathering. William Allis is returning from Ceylon!" He fell silent momentarily, and then resumed, emphatically: "William Allis! Oh, Monsieur, that's the man it's necessary for you to know. An ascetic, a pure yogi, a saint already absorbed in God's infinity. Yes, yes. Monsieur Jaucort, it's necessary to see him and hear him. Tomorrow, Madame de Planor and I are going to dinner at the Père's house in the Avenue Suchet, in the Ranelagh. Come, a little before seven. We'll introduce you, he'll invite you, your conversion will be completed, and the cause of our God will count a new defender, you, one illustrious among men!"

Nonplussed by his familiar manners, I did not know what response to make; the ridiculousness of my situation embarrassed me, and yet I felt very emotional.

"It's agreed, then," the individual insisted. "Tomorrow at seven, at the Allis house, Avenue Suchet, in the Ranelagh. Do you know the Ranelagh well?"

Of course I knew the Ranelagh, and the entire past of that little corner of our Parisian suburbs, and that old engraving that made me smile so much every day—the same one whose frame had gleamed so fantastically the previous evening. That square in Passy was one of my favorite walks. I stammered, nevertheless, a few words of excuse, and made as if to withdraw.

"Pierrette!" called Monsieur de Planor.

A red-faced and pug-nosed little maidservant immediately came running, wearing the dress with velvet decorations and the mitered bonnet of Breton women.

"Pierrette," said her master, "go announce to Madame the visit of Monsieur René Jaucourt.

With a hieratic gesture he extended his hand over the red hair of the country wench, and in the tone of a confessor, he said: "What supererogatory proof have you endured today, my child?"

The paltry creature rolled frightened eyes, and stammered a few idiotic words. All day long she had not eaten in response to her hunger, because of the holy desire to mortify her flesh.

Monsieur de Planor approved, nodding his head blissfully. "Good, very good, my dear girl! But that isn't sufficient. It's necessary to know how to crucify oneself more, to expiate for our anterior lives even more than for our present life. Now, Pierrette, announce Monsieur."

Then, taking the arm of the medium Aleph, and without waiting for my response, the extravagant old man drew away. I followed them with my gaze for some time; they were both walking at a precipitate pace, like people spurred by time, demanded by an imperious duty. Finally, at the corner of the Rue Breda, they stopped a fiacre and disappeared.

In truth, the mysterious abode of Monsieur de Planor intrigued me keenly: artistic curiosity. I went in. The vestibule into which I penetrated initially had lost its ornamental character. Imbecile hands had torn away the wood paneling in order to lay the wall bare. Over the whiteness of an ignoble plaster, theurgical inscriptions ran hither and yon, borrowed either from the Vedas or the excessively famous Welsh triads. They were translated into French and I read a few of them rapidly:

> *The man who has chosen the beyond arrives at the supreme absorption from which one no longer descends down here. The man who had chosen the earth must reenter a maternal womb in order to be incarnated again in an earthly body.*
>
> Veda-Vyasa.

> *By virtue of three things a man falls back into the necessity of Abred (Hell on Earth): the absence of effort toward knowledge; the misunderstanding of good and the practice of evil.*
>
> Iolo Morganwg, *Bardic Triads*

To the right and left two large doors were facing one another. On one a commercial placard was displayed: *Redemption: Editorial Office.* The other gave access to some mysterious room. It was painted black, and symbolic signs were outlined in red on each batten: the Alpha-Omega of the Byzantines and, lower down, a word in a language unknown to me: *Aum.*

Dark velvet curtains trimmed with gold framed that portal, thus completing a comically funereal aspect.

"What's that?" I asked Pierrette, who was preceding me. She blinked, shrugged her shoulders and replied. In a mocking tone: "The Sanctuary, my good Monsieur . . . their parish, you might say."

"They celebrate rites there?"

"Yes, indeed! Masses and vespers, in their fashion: funny ones. The master plays the rector there, and the other, the Englishman, Allis, is his bishop."

With that, the reincarnate scullion—some king's daughter, perhaps—uttered a loud burst of laughter.

At the extremity of the vestibule was the stairwell. Still guided by the Bretonne, I had begun to climb it when I stopped, gripped. On the first floor someone was singing: a woman's voice rose up in the silence. I listened; the inexpressible emotion that had oppressed me the previous day had just seized me again.

Yes, yes, I had heard it before, that vibrant voice. It was the same one that had disturbed my heart twice, once in the chapel of Saint-Sulpice, and yesterday in the Boulevard Saint-Germain. Accompanying herself on the piano, she was singing Dalayrac's melody, my ballad: the appeal to the Beloved, a passionate, despairing sob, a reckless cry toward the ideal; one might have thought the woman was putting her entire soul into her voice.

I looked at my watch: it marked ten o'clock—the very moment when I had heard it the previous evening, in the solitude of my cabinet. Quite bizarre!

"Who is that singing?" I asked Pierrette.

"Madame."

"Is she alone?"

"All alone. Every evening she shuts herself in her room to sing and to weep. Oh, the poor woman isn't happy!"

I took out my visiting card and held it out to the indiscreet girl. "Ask Madame de Planor whether she will accord me the honor of receiving me."

The maidservant climbed up to the first floor, briskly. A few moments went by in expectation. The voice fell silent. Then, after one or two silent minutes, Pierrette came back down.

"Madame is suffering," she said, "and cannot receive Monsieur."

I was shown out. Involuntarily chagrined, I retraced my steps, scolding myself and swearing never again to cross the threshold of that misbegotten house. What had I to do there, and what stupidity had led me to take the previous evening's banal invitation seriously? What did the Frères-unis matter to me, with their sanctuary, their pontiffs, their karma and that lugubrious carnival of grotesque buffoonery?

Cursing fate, I had already traversed the length of the vestibule when an extravagant inspiration—where had it come from?—crossed my mind. Taking out my portfolio I tore out a page and scribbled a few lines on it in pencil:

> *You're refusing to receive me, but I must speak to you. Tomorrow, you're going to dinner with William Allis. At six o'clock I shall be waiting in the square of the Ranelagh, near the entrance to the Bois de Boulogne.*

I even dared to underline the phrase: *I must speak to you.*

"Take that to Madame de Planor," I said to the chambermaid, who went away for a second time.

This time, the wait was not long. Almost immediately, the redhead came back and said insolently: "Here's the response." At the same time, she tipped the pieces of my note, torn to sheds, into my hands. Madame de Planor had not deigned to make any other response to my unwelcome letter; I had therefore to leave. In any case, a reaction had just taken place within me; I was ashamed of my conduct, and I did not understand how a man of my education had been able to commit such an ignominy. What! Was I going mad myself, and was the insanity of the house contagious? I did not know her at all, this Madame de Planor, and I dared to write to her like a beloved seen again after a long absence! She must have laughed.

Without asking any more, I launched myself outside, and the Bretonne shot the bolts loudly behind me.

The sky had cleared; now it was scintillating, iridescent with stars. I was going along the street at a rapid pace when, having reached a bend in the road, I turned round with a mechanical movement. Then, under the whiteness spread by the moon, on the first floor of that house of dementia, I perceived open shutters, and the motionless form of a woman who, her head extended, was gazing at me.

V

Of all suburban walks, the one my idling prefers in April is still the verdant and perfumed Ranelagh. There, in that pleasant quarter of a restful suburb, among the cottages and the villas, a Parisian can forget Paris for an hour. Under the foliage of its old trees there are no deafening crowds and very few loiterers: the silence of others and the calm of oneself. In summer, however, the dreamer has to go somewhere else to shade his reveries, for he is no longer alone and banal rumors deafen and enervate him. On the grass trampled by boule players, military bands play their brass instruments; babies wail and mothers jabber, housewives gossip and those yet to marry make eyes. The Ranelagh then presents all the horrors of Sunday in a small provincial town. But in April, everything is still human silence there and the birds are already twittering; the chestnut trees raise the thyrses of their crowns pompously; the lawns dapple their green carpets with yellow and white; the heady fragrance of acacias intoxicates you and make you drowsy; a flowery solitude in which melancholy spring, so full of hope and tender quietude, expands languidly.

It was after six o'clock when I went into the shady pathway that goes round the Ranelagh and extends toward the Auteuil railway. It is rather profound, very leafy, and stretches out darkly in the enveloping light of day. I had come, guided by habit, idle and sulky, dissatisfied with myself and still under the emotion of the previous evening's escapade. Oh, how the slightest sensations traversed that day were still present in my memory! Enervating anxieties were agitating me: the ennui of my solitary life; a dolorous desire to love and be loved. April caused the most mysterious frissons to pass through me.

While walking slowly, I recited cadences of prose to myself, and improvised verses with splendid rhymes. I listened to the silence and gazed into space . . .

Suddenly, my heart leapt and I began to walk more rapidly. At the extremity of the avenue, in the distance, near the entrance to the Bois de Boulogne, I glimpsed a form, an as-yet-indecisive silhouette: a woman. She went back and forth, sat down on a bench, stood up immediately and appeared to be waiting, impatient and agitated. Abruptly, she advanced toward me, and abruptly, I launched myself toward her. I had recognized her. Madeleine!

Madeleine? I had a moment of doubt, however, and thought it was an illusion. The woman was dressed in black and her lowered veil hid her face from me. A few seconds went by before she joined me, and during those brief instants, I thought I lived the whole long extent of a human life. Anguish, hope, joy and wellbeing invaded me by turns, succeeding one another . . .

Yes, it was really her. Quivering, Madame de Planor stopped and, lifting her veil, showed me all the pallor of her face.

"Here I am," she said. "What do you want with me?"

Her speech was curt and dry, her eyes brilliant, her movements jerky, the muscles of her face taut and rigid; one might have thought her a somnambulist traversing the ecstasies of hypnosis. Emotion strangled me, and at first I could make no response. Finally, with a reckless gesture, I seized her hands, and inclined my head passionately toward the fingers.

"I love you!" I stammered. "I love you! Oh . . . forgive me!"

She recoiled, as if terrified. "No, no, it's necessary not to love me! Have pity on me! Have pity on yourself!"

Certainly, I knew, for having heard it many times, that deceptive cry of a woman hastening to her first rendezvous. I therefore bowed, smiling. But Madame de Planor's dolorous voice had caused me some surprise—and there was not a word of reproach for the indelicacy of my conduct, nor any excuse for the inconsequence of her coming. I was seeing her there for the first time, and yet one might have thought that she was accustomed to our encounters.

Now we were walking side by side, heading toward the Bois.

At the exit from the Porte de Passy one can see, opening to the right, a discreet and winding path. It is a slender zigzag, which goes around the rampart and along the sinuosities of the counter-slope: on one side, there are the depths of the moat, and the ditch, now a seed-nursery; on the other, a thorny thicket of trees and brushwood. The abandonment of that winding path attracted me; in that lost corner, I was sure, we would not encounter anyone. I indicated it to Madame de Planor and, followed by her, I went into the pathway. The narrowness of the path had brought us closer together, and I felt my companion's shoulder brush mine at times.

Then I looked at the young woman and I admired the distinguished oval of her face, the slimness of her figure, the decent elegance of her costume: everything, including a modest bouquet of white violets pinned to her bodice. Very gently, I put my arm under the elbow of her arm, and, with a weak embrace, held her against my breast. She shivered, and smiled in a distressed fashion, but without repelling my caress. And we walked thus, at a slow pace, almost enlaced, silently.

The azure of the sky extended, light and limpid; the sun, already declining, seemed to me to be full of joy; the evening breeze was beginning to blow, and at that hour of the evening, the Bois sent us the great murmur of its songs.

Madame de Planor was the first to break the voluptuous silence.

"So, you love me?" she said, sadly. "Me, a stranger, you love me?"

"Yes, I love you," I replied, unable to make any other reply, and edifying phrases rapidly. "I love you with a sudden and violent amour. Why? I don't know. Perhaps the thunderbolt of which our poets speak. But what does the cause of the sudden passion matter, since I love you?"

She listened pensively, approving with a smile and caressing me with her gaze.

"Yes, yes, that's it: the thunderbolt of which your poets sing. But that grandiose word doesn't explain anything, Monsieur. It's necessary to look further for the meaning of this enigma, the revelation of a holy mystery."

She fell silent momentarily; then, simultaneously timid and flirtatious: "You ought to be very scornful of me, Monsieur, for having come so quickly to your rendezvous. However, I swear to you that I'm neither an adventuress nor a fallen woman."

I seized her hand, and my only response was to kiss it ardently. But immediately, as at our first meeting, she uttered a faint cry and, with a dolorous gesture, withdrew her hand.

"No, no! For pity's sake, no! You kiss burns me; it makes me feel very ill."

I looked at her, surprised. She was serious, and genuinely seemed to be in pain. Then, having become strangely solemn: "You haven't read it, then, Monsieur? Or rather, you're refusing to understand?"

"Read . . . what?" I said.

"The book that Monsieur de Planor gave you . . . the account of his doctrines . . . the formidable theory of karma?"

I was astounded. That ludicrous question, that sudden allusion to the imbecility of the Frères-unis had just thrown a discordant note between us. Now, I thought I divined that I must be alas, the victim of some ridiculous enterprise. Informed of my absurd escapade, Monsieur de Planor had sent his wife to me, perhaps hoping to exploit my stupidity and thus make me one of the catechumens of his chapel. With fanatics of that species, was not anything presumable? Good God! A fine adventure! A chagrined anger seized me, and I shrugged my shoulders disdainfully.

"Yes, I read it," I replied, "and I attempted to comprehend; but in order to believe in your karma, I'll wait until I'm interned in some lunatic asylum."

The young woman looked at me again, alarmed. "Don't mock!" she exclaimed. "You and I are subject to it, this karma."

"You're the most charming of missionaries," I continued, amused by her fear, "but admit it, you've only come here with the agreement of your husband."

An indignant blush spread over the pallor of her face. "Oh, what an abject thought! My husband is a very honest man, Monsieur, an apostle, and, if necessary, he would be a martyr."

"My compliments. And this martyr, this apostle, this perfect gallant man loves you?"

"Passionately."

"And you, dear Madame?"

She lowered her eyes, bowed her head; then, slowly, in a very low voice: "If I loved him, would I be here?"

Meanwhile, dusk was falling. Spring mists were exuding from the ground, still moist, a floating grayness that spread around us. Under their confused vapors, the path was effaced, outlines lost their contours, and in the thickets the trees loomed up gigantically; the profundities became immense. We had both resumed walking, silent again. At that pious moment of falling night, I felt myself invaded by a religious disturbance. The mortified bitterness that had rendered me bad-tempered a little while ago gave way now to sensations of an infinite softness.

I still suspected Monsieur de Planor of some extravagant calculation, but I acquired the tenderness of amour for the young woman so ingenuously abandoned to my honor.

"Madeleine! Dear Madeleine!"

And, with a passionate movement, I dared to put my arm around her waist. She inclined her head on to my shoulder, and for a split second I shivered under the caress of that burden. But she straightened up very quickly and pulled away from my embrace; a strange abruptness had just succeeded her languor. A tremor agitated her spasmodically; she fixed her eyes on the mirages of the fog and gazed as if in ecstasy.

"If I were a novelist like you," she said, "I would like to recount the confused sensations of two souls finally rediscovering one another after a century of absence . . . here, for example . . . in a solitude repopulated by memory . . . on an exactly similar evening of renewal. The aspect of this place is much changed. Once, the Bois de Boulogne extended all the way to Passy; the Ranelagh and its fashionable concert were only a crossroads in the forest. It was a pleasure then to see the luminous chain of Venetian lanterns trembling under the foliage, to hear the rhythmic cadence of gavottes vibrating in the distance, to listen in one's lover's arms to the melodies of a Méhul or a Dalayrac.

When the beloved returns
To his languishing friend . . .

"Ah! If one of the amorous beauties who gave their gallant rendezvous here returned to life, could she really recognize it?"

I stopped, amazed. How had she divined my intimate thought like that, the subject of my mystical novel on which I had been working for long months in vain? And how, above all, had she described so well the engraving that . . .

But I did not have time to interrogate her; suddenly, she uttered a faint cry of fright. In the blackness of the thicket I glimpsed a human form, which was marching some distance away and following us, step for step: doubtless some prowler of the wood, one of those vagabonds who sleep under the stars.

"Allis!" stammered Madame de Planor.

She seemed terrified. The increasing shadow hid her face from me, but I felt her arm trembling under mine. I strove to reassure her: such a pursuit was too implausible.

"What kind of man is he, your Monsieur Allis?" I asked.

She hesitated momentarily before replying, but finally, lowering her voice further, she said: "A terrible man!"

It was necessary for us to separate. Traversing the Ranelagh again, I accompanied Madame de Planor as far as the first houses of the Avenue Suchet; but there she was seized by her terrors again.

"No, no!" she said. "I won't go to that man's house this evening; he would only have to look at me to divine everything." And she added, bowing her head: "I would be telling a lie—my first lie!"

A few carriages were parked outside the railway station. She took one of them. I leaned on the door.

"When shall I see you again . . . Madeleine?"

She did not reply. I went on, imploring: "Oh, come back, I beg you! Soon, no? Tomorrow!"

VI

And the next day, I was at the rendezvous; she came back on the days that followed. Then there were daily encounters in the solitudes of certain remote districts, sometimes in the propitious avenues that envelop the low quarters of Auteuil, sometimes on the bleak boulevards that extend alongside the Parc de Montsouris. But the "precursor of summer" had now arrived and the importunate length of the days constrained us to move our shepherd's hour much later.

I was sometimes astonished by that complete liberty left to a young woman, and at times the suspicion reentered my mind of a connivance with her husband.

"You have your midnight pass every evening, then, Madeleine?"

She smiled, always enigmatic, but the candor of the smile reassured me rapidly.

In any case, Monsieur de Planor had just departed on a "pastoral excursion" in company with William Allis, "the terrible man." He had gone to visit a small church of the Frères-unis recently founded on the shores of Lake Geneva, at Montreux, in the heart of Vaudois Protestantism. Those amusing sectarians were beginning to pullulate and spread through the world. They could be encountered in France, Switzerland, Germany, Norway,

England, India and America; the reign of the Eternal Now was imminent.

Nevertheless, while awaiting the advent of the day of days, those messieurs were threatened with losing one of their souls of election: Madame de Planor herself. As our encounters multiplied, the mystical "sister," the believer in karma, disappeared, giving way to a simple amorous woman. The flesh of the reincarnate began to quiver, the woman rediscovered herself . . .

And every evening, while we walked along the tenebrous avenues, pressed against one another, so happily, we talked. Madeleine told me about her youth, the story of her marriage, and the disillusionments and ennuis of her conjugal life. She was Irish, raised in Paris, and her early years had been spent in a modest apartment in the vicinity of the Luxembourg. Her father, a man named Fitzpatrick, a worthy man devoid of a fortune, had married when his youth had passed a lady of the old Breton nobility, very rich, and a high dignitary in the church of the Frères-unis. Brought up in baroque ideas of occultism, she confessed that her faith had long been ardent, but was now lukewarm. Monsieur de Planor, in any case, was a crackpot, spending a large fortune in propagating his folly, recruiting followers everywhere, even daring to but conversions. Yes, but a loyal soul, a very honest man, and also a very literate man. He held my books in a singular esteem, having read them and having made his young wife, his disciple, read them.

"It's such a long time that I've been living close to you," she said to me one day. "I ought to have fled, but I wanted to see again."

"See again, Madeleine?"

"Hasn't it ever happened to you, my friend, in traveling through some unknown land to feel yourself shudder abruptly? You don't know it, and yet you recognize it. Those woods, those fields, those strands, those mountains, like old companions rediscovered, seem to be bidding you welcome. Listen then to the voice of their silence: 'Here you are, then, returned among us, changing form of an essence always the same, poor divine sinner, fallen and vagabond, immortal dead-alive! Look: here you were happy, and there you suffered. Salutations! The eyes of your body have been able to pass before us blindly, but your soul has recognized us, since it has shuddered; your heart has retained our memory, since it is full of tears. Yes, the secret of your melancholy, distressed soul, is the persistence of memory; but is it, alas, a dolor more bitter than being able to forget?'"

At that moment we were crossing the Place Saint-Sulpice. It was the dead of night, and the enormous neo-Greek building stood out more somberly against the azured blackness of the sky. While walking, Madeleine indicated the church to me.

"An old friend, that one," she said. "It was witness to the first delights of my heart; I loved gentle Jesus so sweetly! Why, then, did that naïve faith of the multitude leave my soul forever? When, as a little girl, I lived in one of those back-streets huddled in the shadow of the church, the bell of the angelus woke me up every morning, and it was the angelus again that lulled me to sleep every evening. *Ave Maria!* O merciful mother, bestower of clement smiles, very fortunate is the woman who can believe and immerse herself in you! And later, as a little girl, at the epoch of my first communion, it was at Saint-Sulpice again that I . . . but what's the matter, René, and why is your arm trembling under mine?"

I was in fact, trembling; the emotion of a very distant memory had just gripped me again, and its dear phantom rose up before me again.

"A question, Madeleine! In that epoch, did you follow the exercises of the catechism?"

"Yes, why ask me that?"

"Do you remember one evening in December, twenty-two years ago, Christmas Eve? I came into Saint-Sulpice, deserted at that moment. Children were gathered in the crypt of the church. I couldn't see them but I could hear their voices. A priest was speaking to them and the children were responding by singing canticles. Were you among them, Madeleine?"

"Certainly, without a doubt."

"And that canticle, do you recall it? Naïve words to an old tune by Dalayrac . . . the ballad of 'The Beloved.'"

She squeezed my hand with a reckless embrace. "Oh, René, Rene, you were already so close to me!"

Nevertheless, those mystical transports were becoming rarer by the day in Madeleine. An ardent sensuality was igniting within her, adding a rosiness to her face and a gleam to her gaze. Now, there were fewer words between us than kisses, and the harmonious silence of amorous ecstasies. Everything in the passionate woman that still resisted was voluptuousness for me: the thinning of her face, the febrile brightness of her eyes, the languid abandonment of her stance, her joy, her laughter, her tears, and even her alarms. So reckless in our first meetings, she was now anxious and fearful. An encounter with a passer-by caused her the panic of a child caught at fault.

"Someone's coming! What if he were to recognize me?"

And, like a pusillanimous child, she hid her face against my breast. The man went past us indifferently, and immediately, a nervous laugh succeeded the alarm.

"I'm foolish, my friend; you're going to find me ridiculous . . . but I thought I perceived William Allis."

Again and again, that same name recurred in her terrors.

Often, too, the chimes of a clock informed us that it was late and that our walk had gone on too long. Then Madeleine became madly agitated.

"Eleven o'clock already! What will they think of me? I'm doomed. I don't want to . . . I mustn't . . . compromise myself like this any longer!"

But the following day, I did not have to wait for her; she was the first to run to our rendezvous.

Those repeated alarms, doubtless in fear of her husband, had dissipated my last suspicions; now, I abandoned myself without mistrust to the illusions of my romance.

Toward the middle of July, Monsieur de Planor returned to Paris. Our encounters became more difficult, and Madeleine soon begged me to renounce evening rendezvous. It was therefore necessary to risk ourselves in broad daylight. I proposed my apartment to shelter our quotidian meetings but she refused, timorously, and I was obliged to rent a pied-à-terre in a remote suburban quarter. She came to it, not without reluctance, and there, in the banal bedroom of a furnished house, she became entirely mine for the first time.

Every afternoon, now, posted behind a curtain, I lay in wait for her arrival. What anguish there was in my heart while I counted the minutes and seconds impatiently! And what suffocating joy when her carriage finally stopped under my windows! A woman descended, with her veil pulled down, crossed the road rapidly, and I ran to open my door slightly; I heard the rustle of her dress on the stairway, and furtive footsteps; the door was pushed violently, and Madeleine fell into my arms.

Recklessly, I loved her more with every passing day. She had become the companion necessary to my life, my thought, my inspiration and my talent. I had returned to work and I read my morning's labor to her, pages of novels or dramatic scenarios; I listened to her opinions, and followed her advice. With what ardor I now wished for glory, and summoned it, in order to adorn my beloved!

Music further augmented with its enervation the languid ecstasy of our two beings. My beloved sat down at a piano and the mystical masters, Schubert, Mendelssohn, Schumann, and Chopin above all, wept or sang beneath her fingers . . .

And it was thus that Madeleine, today at the limits of her youth, and I, already aging, exhausted to the point of intoxication the wellbeing of amour—the amour that I had long pursued in vain, which I no longer believed to exist on earth, but which I had finally discovered.

VII

In the meantime, autumn had arrived, and was already powdering the russet of our gardens with frost; the November wind withered the last chrysanthemums and caused the faded yellow leaves to rain down.

One day, I waited for Madeleine for a long time; she missed our rendezvous. The next day, the same disappointed expectation: no letter, no telegram; anxiety took possession of me. What was happening? Why had my beloved not written to me? Ought I to believe that she was ill, or had "the other"—her husband—finally become suspicious? An entire week went by in dread, and for interminable hours I remained on tenterhooks, in vain, behind my curtain.

Finally, tortured by anguish and divining some misfortune, I resolved to go in search of news and, if necessary, to force Monsieur de Planor's door.

That evening, therefore, the first of December, in a bitter winter cold—oh, I have piously retained the memory of that lugubrious night!—I set forth for the Rue Notre-Dame-des-Champs. My design was, on the pretext of a visit, to reach Madeleine, to exchange a few words with her, or at least a gaze, and thus to calm my anxiety.

The sky was heavy and dense, without a single star; tenebrous vapors enveloped Paris and an icy mist floated in the blackness of the air. I took a carriage and had myself conducted as far as the crossroads of the Rue Vavin. There, getting down, I perceived that it was snowing: a desolating misfortune. How could I explain my coming in such weather? My heart constricted, with a heavy tread, I went along the Rue Notre-Dame-des-Chaps. The wind lashed my face, but I did not feel its bite. At intervals I stopped to shake off the powdery snow covering my garments, and then resumed my route, even more slowly.

My watch indicated nine o'clock when I arrived at Monsieur de Planor's house. Finally, I was about to know. The door was closed. I stretched out my arm toward the bell, but suddenly, I stopped, hesitantly. A previously-unknown timidity retained my hand. What if I compromised Madeleine by my visit?

I drew away rapidly, only to return immediately, and for long minutes I went back and forth outside the door . . .

It was now half past nine; impossible to present myself: it was too late. No, it was better to remain there, and observe. The street was solitary, and in that snowy torment no passer-by was to be feared. I went to establish myself in the shadow of a wall opposite the house, and I watched.

The house developed its bleak façade in the darkness, punctured here and there by a few lights, but Madeleine's windows remained dark, and their shutters were still open. It was very late, though! Where could she be at such an hour?

Gradually, the lights went out, and a heavy silence weighed upon the slumbering house. Only Monsieur de Planor's bedroom remained illuminated, and an uncertain, flickering yellow light descended therefrom—that of a lamp, or perhaps a night-light. At intervals, I perceived the silhouette of a woman moving back and forth. Her! Madeleine! So she was there . . . there, in that bedroom, her husband's bedroom! And I watched, motionless and covered in snow, shivering but sweating . . .

Eleven o'clock, and midnight chimed, and I did not think of going away; I wanted to know . . .

To know what? A poignant suffering, an atrocious jealousy, caused me to laugh and weep with rage. At times, I extended my arm menacingly: "Aha! I finally know them, your lies, giver of the same kisses to your husband and your lover, conjugal prostitute!"

Abruptly, the windows were obscured. The interior curtains had been drawn. Then I uttered a furious cry; with my fist I hammered on the courtesan's door, and I fled. The snow was still falling, but for a long time, under the torment, I wandered recklessly through the great slumber of Paris.

When, after two hours of vagabondage, I was finally retrenched at home, I collapsed into an armchair, exhausted. A brutal anger, compounded of amorous suffering and revolted pride, was howling in my heart. Oh, the wretched woman! So, in order to appease your husband's suspicions, you abandon yourself to that man every night! Coward! You, my beloved, you, Madeleine, with the long gaze, so candid, the smile so naïve and so sweet! Well, so be it! It's necessary to break! I want it; I must . . .

Break? Yes, but I can make you suffer too, you who inflicted such tortures on me! Suffer as much as me, in your flesh and in your soul! I'll take a mistress . . . no matter whom . . . I'll render the liaison public, I'll display it even before your eyes. Coward! How sweet to stroll, with my arm around the waist of that other beloved, along the same woodland paths that we strolled together, Madeleine! And how voluptuous to embrace her passionately, the other, in the same room from which I expelled you, wretch . . . degradation, debasement of my entire being: your work, creature! Oh, it won't be long. But first, it's necessary to write to you, a letter that will make a blush rise to the pallor of your face, announcing the break to you and all my scorn for your lying amour. Go on! Weep in your turn, coward, coward . . .

I seized a pen and tried to trace a few lines. But then a sob heaved my breast, a flood of tears sprang from my eyes. The pen fell from my fingers; I could not write . . .

"Oh, poor me! And a coward yourself, wretched René!"

Fatigue overwhelmed me; my head inclined on the back of my armchair; my eyes, burned by insomnia, closed. I became somnolent.

Suddenly, a violent trill of the doorbell made me jump. My lamp had gone out while I was dozing, and I found myself in complete darkness. Straightening up in my armchair, listening, I waited for a few moments. Another trill of the bell, even more vibrant, brought me to my feet. I lit a candle and looked at the clock; it marked five o'clock in the morning. Who would dare to present himself at my house at such an hour?

Outside, someone was knocking, with urgent blows. My domestic was belated in going downstairs. Impatiently, I took a candlestick and headed for the door.

"Who's there?" I demanded.

"Open up!" an imperious voice replied. "Monsieur de Planor is dying, and I've come to fetch you."

VIII

It was a man about forty years old, his hair still very brown, tall and broad-shouldered. His pale face, sun-tanned, like that of a mulatto or a Hindu, was harsh but handsome, in spite of the excessively aquiline curve of the nose. His large eyes announced intelligence, and his already denuded forehead had to contain thought. Long hair brushed backwards, a clean-shaven face, a clergyman's frock-coat and a white cravat gave the individual all the appearance of a Methodist pastor. He crossed the threshold of my door, took a step into the vestibule, and then stopped. Still holding my candlestick in my hand, I looked at the unknown visitor with astonishment.

"I'm William Allis," he said to me, finally.

William Allis! The missionary of the spiritist community, the apostolic initiator of gentiles, the "terrible man" of whom Madeleine spoke fearfully. So this was him! I was seeing him for the first time; his arrogant manner and theatrical pose displeased me immediately.

He looked me up and down brazenly. "Monsieur de Planor is dying," he repeated, "so I've come to fetch you."

I put my candle down on a table and, although very emotional, affected indifference.

"But I scarcely know Monsieur de Planor," I said.

The individual looked me full in the face, and started to laugh: a silent, ironic, insolent laugh.

"You scarcely know him, my dear Monsieur Jaucourt? Bah! For seven months you've been his wife's lover."

He had pronounced the last words in a tone so scornful that anger rose to my lips; I would gladly have slapped him, the boor.

"You dare to say, Monsieur . . . ? Get out!"

He stepped back into the doorway, still looking at me, still keeping his gaze fixed on mine, and in the penumbra of the antechamber I perceived, like a phosphorescent glow, the bizarre gleam of his immobile eyes . . .

What happened within me? I don't know—but, seized by a sudden dazzle, I lowered my gaze and bowed my head.

"Let's go!" he said, then.

And I went with him.

A carriage was waiting for us. William Allis took his place therein beside me. The snowstorm had calmed down, and lunar splendors were now displayed in the heavens, rendering the whiteness spread over Paris whiter still; the finishing night was as bright as a twilight.

My head half-turned toward my companion, I examined him with a bitter curiosity. A Hindu, surely, that taciturn individual with the bronzed face, the frightful and sinister mask, that *vultus mala physionomia* described so often by demonographers.[1]

He was silent, disdainful, abandoning himself indifferently to the indiscretions of my gaze, but I had difficulty sustaining my anxiety. What imprudence on Madeleine's part to choose such a confidant! And by what mysterious peril was she menaced, to send him in quest of me like this? For it was surely her, and her alone, who had sent that man to me; I was certain of it, since I was hastening.

I was the first who wanted to break the painful silence.

"Monsieur de Planor is very ill, then?" I asked, timidly.

---

1 The Latin phrase simply means "nasty-looking face"; I can find no evidence of it being used frequently by demonographers.

William Allis shrugged his shoulders. "He's going to die. A lesion in the heart. It's chagrin that is killing him. But what does the name of his malady matter? He has accomplished the time of his ordeal; he is liberating himself."

The arrogant individual fell silent momentarily, and then resumed in a dry and harsh tone: "You would have been apprised of it twelve days ago, Monsieur; the adulterous wife wrote to you many times. I intercepted the letters."

"What! You have dared . . . !" I cried, menacingly

The same disdainful laughter grimaced in his mouth again. "Yes, I have dared. The wretched woman gave you a rendezvous a few steps from the house where her husband lay dying. An ignominy! I wanted to spare you both a shame and a remorse." And, speaking to himself, he added: "In any case, the day of redemption is about to break for her."

We arrived in the Rue Notre-Dame-des-Champs. The bleak and somber house was still closed. William Allis knocked on the door, gently, and Pierrette came to open it.

"Monsieur no longer recognizes anyone," she murmured.

"He will recognize me," Allis told her. "Have the Brothers that I summoned arrived?"

"They're here."

Seven or eight men were grouped in the vestibule: bizarre heads, bearded, with unkempt hair, doubtless the potentates of the little theurgical church: mages, hierophants, sârs, epopts, pandects and yogis. All clad in black, they were talking in low voices. Allis marched toward them and a profound silence immediately fell.

"My children," he said to them, in a tender voice, "a human dolor is about to attain us, but at the same time, a celestial joy will dry up our tears. Our beloved brother, the expiator Jean de Planor, is completing at this moment the proof of his last incarnation; he is escaping the earth. Heavy as the burden of his karma has been, he has supported it valiantly. What am I saying?

He has even imposed a voluntary dolor upon himself, the cruelest of our Vedantic *tapas*—and he is dying of it . . .

"Poor, poor friend, go, the clement mildness of the Eternal Now will receive you in its mercy; I hope, I know, I affirm it. Tomorrow, Planor will inhabit a star. We, however, his family, his disciples, while the combat of his death-throes lasts, let us pray. I prescribe, for the moment, the orison epsilon of our ritual. But as soon as the soul has broken its chain, let a canticle of hosannah flying from our lips rise with the rising soul, into space, into the ether, toward the light, toward the infinity of God. Go, then, my children; devote yourselves to prayer."

And with a gesture, William Allis designated to his "children," the bearded and hirsute sârs, the open door of the "sanctuary." He closed it behind them, and approached me.

"You, Monsieur," he said, "come."

A strange malaise gradually overtook me, however; a torpor numbed my will, almost bewildering me. I was rational nevertheless, and I tried to react. Why, then, had I followed that man, that charlatan, that grotesque, that clown? To preserve Madeleine from some divined peril . . . Dear, dear Madeleine! How I had calumniated you a little while ago! So, my beloved, the silhouette of the woman glimpsed in the night was not that of an adulterous lover, but that of a nurse inclining over the bed of a dying man. Even at that moment, your thought was appealing to me; you were suffering from my silence! And this unworthy Allis dared to intercept your letters! Oh, you, evil clown, demonic figure I shall be able to punish you some day!

The voice of the prophet spoke rudely to me, even harsher and drier: "Let's go up. It's high time."

"Inform Madame," I replied, "that I am waiting for her here."

He shook his head disdainfully. "She will not come."

"What! Was it not her who sent you?"

"No."

"Who was it, then?"

"Her husband."

Her husband! I stepped back a few paces, stupefied. William Allis rejoined me and placed his hand on my shoulder. "Are you afraid?" he said, insolently

His voice and his gaze expressed such scorn that I was ashamed of my weakness. A trap? I would be able to get out of it. And then, Madeleine must be in that mortuary chamber, under insult and perhaps threat. I did not hesitate any longer.

"Let's go, Monsieur. I'm yours."

The chamber whose door William Allis opened was only feebly illuminated. Acrid pharmaceutical odors filled it, vitiating the atmosphere, and to begin with, I thought I might suffocate. In a corner of the room I perceived, drowned in shadow, a modest iron bed, and, on the narrow mattress a rigid form, motionless in the covers. A dolorous crepitation, already very weak, exhaled from the recumbent body; a little more time and the moribund individual's death-rattle would cease.

Near the bed, collapsed in an armchair, a woman seemed to be asleep: Madeleine. At the sound made by the door, she lifted her head, and came to her feet abruptly.

"Madeleine," William Allis said to her. "It's Monsieur Jaucourt. He wanted to come. He had to."

Madame de Planor uttered a frightened cry, tottered, and then fell back into her armchair, as if knocked down. No, she was certainly not expecting me.

"You, Monsieur," Allis went on, "approach, and have no fear; there is nothing here but forbearance and pity."

Paused on the threshold of the room, preparing myself for some sinister adventure, I looked at Madeleine. She turned imploring eyes toward me and made a gesture, as if to summon me. I approached . . .

Now the glow of a night-light permitted me to make out the dying man's features: his hollow and jaundiced cheeks, his soiled beard, his lips, where a few drops of blood had pearled, his fixed and vitreous pupils, his forehead bathed with sweat; and something—I know not what—in the agonizing body, was already soothing his suffering, although he had not yet entered into the impassive mildness of the great dreamless sleep.

At that moment, from the floor below, the modulations of a harmonium rose up, accompanying a canticle. In the sanctuary, the assembled brethren had begun a prayer, and they were chanting to a monotonous music, in cadenced prose, like some liturgical psalmody.

> *Day is breaking, come to me;*
> *Without you I cannot live;*
> *Night is falling, come to me;*
> *Without you I dare not die!*

At the rhythm of that chant, Monsieur de Planor seemed to shudder, and his arms, extends on the coverlet, agitated. William Allis leaned over him, and said to him in an affectionate tone: "Jean, it's me, William, your disciple, the child of your thought; do you recognize me? Yes? And here's Madeleine, your companion in the proof, your wife according to the flesh. Do you recognize her?"

The head that was rigid on the pillow was raised feebly; the extinct eyes gleamed; a tear ran over the creases of the face, and like the fingers of a blind man seeking and groping, the clenched fingers opened, groping and searching. William Allis took Madeleine's hand and placed it under her husband's hand.

"Jean," he continued, "you loved her very much, and you still love her. Do you want to forgive her?"

Then the dying mouth slackened, and, like a sobbing plaint, the confused sound of a word—only one—reached me.

"The *other?*"

"Here he is!" said Allis. "Forgive again."

He seized my hand and placed it in Madeleine's . . . under the grip of mercy. A faint pressure announced to us that, henceforth united by the husband himself, the adulterous wife and lover were pardoned.

"And now," murmured William Allis, "go to sleep in the peace of your Lord. You have just won the most beautiful victory, and your karma no longer exists. Soul of light, launch yourself gloriously toward the light!"

A sigh, perhaps the last, responded to him. And the two of us—she and I—remained united for a long time by the contraction of the supreme embrace.

The voice of William Allis finally broke that funereal charm.

"He's dead," he told me. "Now, Monsieur, you can go."

I looked at Madeleine, but she turned her eyes away in order not to see me. Once again I squeezed her hand. Then, silently, head bowed, with slow steps, I left.

Day had broken: a livid dawn, the glacial sunrise of a December morning . . .

. . . .

And a week went by, rapid for me, even, if I dare say it, almost joyful. The sad impression of the funereal night had been rapidly effaced from my memory—or rather, I only retained one memory from it: Madeleine was mine—mine forever.

The newspapers informed me of a few details of Monsieur de Planor's obsequies, but very briefly and in a mocking tone: a civil burial escorted by women dressed in white and men with flowers in their buttonholes; over the tomb, many speeches, verse and prose; then, after the ceremony, an Etruscan banquet. In brief, all the gaiety of a petty shopgirl's wedding, a funeral conducted joyfully, as befitted the joyful *exitus* of a soul heading for the stars.

Impatience, however, was beginning to agitate me, and soon I appealed with all my desire to the hour when I could decently present myself before my friend, my fiancée, my wife. I had become very timid, and I was waiting for a note from her authorizing my visit. Three more days passed.

Finally, on the morning of the twelfth day, I received a letter . . . from Madeleine. But it bore a foreign stamp! Posted in Brindisi!

Frightened, I tore open the envelope.

The letter only contained a single word:

Adieu.

✳

(Here there is a profound lacuna in René Jaucourt's manuscript. Several leaves are left blank; others, overladen with erasures, have become illegible. The story, however, resumes a few pages further on, but in an unexpected form: that of a journal in a tormented style, sometimes even incorrect, surely the work of a sick man.)

IX

20 February 1890. I'm saved; inclement death did not want me.

This morning, my dear old comrade Legaux declared that I have just entered into convalescence. A cerebral fever! What an excellent fellow Martial Legaux is, and how savant and devoted. How was I able to misunderstand his merit and calumniate his character? For an entire week he has been at my bedside, lavishing care, despairing and desperate. I've been so very ill, I'm told. A cerebral fever!

The fit seized me abruptly one evening, as I was finishing writing the story of a lamentable amorous adventure—mine, I believe . . . yes, mine. Oh, my memory is very weak, and opaque fogs are floating heavily over my thought. But I'm no longer suffering.

"Well, my poor friend," Legaux exclaimed, "all's well that ends well, but damn it, I feared momentarily for your reason!"

Madness! With the perpetual sweetness of dream and the endless sensuality of illusion! What bliss that must be, O my soul!

✳

22 February. A newspaper has, it appears, announced my "complete recovery," and this morning's post brought me a thick wad of letters. I read a few of them, at random: banalities, pure formulae of polite indifference; I'm congratulated on my fortunate cure. Fortunate! I looked at the handwriting of the others; then, without even opening the envelopes, I shoved them all pell-mell into a drawer. Where, then, is the letter so desired that I await every day, and which doesn't arrive?

23 February. Madeleine! Oh, Madeleine!

24 February. Memory is gradually returning, and I must be completely cured now, since I remember and feel myself weeping. The letter so much desired, Madeleine's second letter, reached me a long time ago, and it was reading it that made me faint. I was found lying on the floor unconscious, and it was then that the fever declared itself, the delirium and the brief dementia. I thought that letter lost, but I've found it, and I want to transcribe it. With what delight I shall feel quivering under my hand each of the words that quivered under yours, my beloved!

> *Aboard the India Mail* Prince Albert,
> *quitting Europe.*

> *When you receive this letter, my love, I shall be far away from you. Allis, today the chief of the religion to which I belong, and ordained in the name of the Eternal, commands that I expiate. I must, I want to expiate—for me and for you. May the infinite clemency of the Merciful, accepting my sacrifice, dissolve the*

skepticism of your heart, open your eyes to the sublime light, and then grant our liberated souls the enlacements of immortal amour!

I loved you from the first day; fleeing you, I love you; dying, I shall love you still. Why, then, the strange suddenness of that delirium? Why that sudden and overwhelming passion? I know, now, and it is time that a ray of light fallen from on high illuminates you in your turn. Once united with one another—I cannot doubt that now—in an anterior existence, having then accepted the sin, we have been put in one another's presence again. The bounty of the One who chastises, but regenerates, has invited us to redemption via dolor, but we were not able to comprehend.

We have resumed the terrestrial pilgrimage at the point where we left it, and sin, alas, has continued the sin. Instead of plunging ourselves into all the expiatory voluptuousness of amorous suffering—the amour without weakness and without sin—we have been cowardly, vile and carnal, you as my lover, me as your mistress: a shameful adventure, in which only my husband has shown himself grandiose. He knew everything, and he forgave everything. For him, the victory is complete, and his death was a triumphant entry into immortality. But can we, my friend, accept the disdain of such a pardon, and is it not time that the lover and the mistress rose to the height of the outraged husband?

Do not seek to see me again down here; my precautions have been taken; you will not be able to discover my retreat. Only know that I am going toward a proof that ought, in purifying me, wash awash our sin, and that I hope soon to leave behind in the mire of earth all the corruption of my body. Courage, my René, for, when the proof is accomplished, I will return close to you. Poor friend, you too are going to suffer, but suffering for the person one loves is loving more . . . and then, what would our terrestrial existence have been henceforth, under the burden of shameful memories, with the crushing pity of Monsieur de Planor weighing on both our consciences? A frightful continuous torture. In any case, your Madeleine, René, already feels very old; and can love, in men like you, long survive the youth of the woman who has charmed them? Alas, no, too fragile hearts! But I love, and I want to be loved; and when I have soon put on the indescribable charm of immortal youth, I shall be able to constrain you to the perpetuity of immortal amour. Then, every reverie of your days and every dream of your nights will be of me—nothing but me! Then, oh then, the delirious ecstasy of relentless passion and endless transports!

Listen, then, and understand me. As soon as my liberated soul has discarded its body, my first visitation will be for you. In whatever place on earth you might be at that moment, I shall hasten to rejoin you. Do you recall the customary caress that made me quiver with pleasure when your lips, posing on my forehead, then went to seek my lips? Well, it is me who, at that blessed moment of return, enlacing you in my arms, will give you that long, long, nuptial kiss. Under the infinite softness of that caress you will understand that your Madeleine has returned to your side.

Au revoir, *then, my lover for eternity, and wait for me. Recklessly, in a sob, I am sending myself to you entirely!*

Your friend, your beloved, your sister, your companion, your wife,

The penitent Madeleine

❋

25 February. William Allis, bandit!

26 February. Is Madeleine right, and does the apparent insanity of spiritism contain a doctrine informing us of a great mystery? The revelation of supraterrestrial things has always been mocked by the imbecility of sages. "The madman on the cross!" people say, in jest . . . and that madman was called Jesus of Nazareth. The occult surrounds us, envelops us and enlaces us with its as-yet-impenetrable darkness. We are atoms in unconscious agitation, which an invisible hand is guiding to their destiny. Why life and why death? Which of our rational philosophers is able to tell us that? Perhaps the naïve theory of karma is absurd, but like old Tertullian I am beginning to believe it, by virtue of its very absurdity.

27 February. This morning, for more than an hour, I remained pensive before the engraving hanging in my study, the libertine engraving of the eighteenth century. A banal subject: old bourgeois Gallicism. Why, then, has that image always caused me such emotion? Why was the garden of the Ranelagh chosen for our first rendezvous? Why the white violets? And why, my love, after detaching that picture, have I passionately placed my lips upon it?

28 February. Today I risked my first convalescent excursion. The weather was dry, cold and bitter, but the gilded whiteness of the sun rendered the azure of the sky joyful. "A one-hour promenade," Legaux said to me, "and above all, in a carriage!" Bah, physician, to the dogs with your medicine, as Macbeth says.[1] I walked toward the Rue Royale, desirous of finally seeing the dear asphalt of the boulevards again.

How is it, then, that I suddenly found myself in the Rue Notre-Dame-des-Champs?

The house had an air of sinister abandonment; the door was shut, the shutters closed. I rang; no response. Further appeal; same silence. I seized the knocker of sculpted iron—pretty Louis XV ironmongery—and started to hammer frantically. Nothing. Finally, attracted by the racket, a policeman came toward me and said: "That's a fine racket. You're wasting your time; the house is empty."

"How can it be empty? Isn't it here that the Frères-unis meet?"

"Who are your Frères-unis? All those jokers who make the dead return? Decamped! The quarter complained and the police closed the shop."

5 March. My unique hope of being able to find Madeleine has gone. William Allis has disappeared. I wanted to talk to that man to move him to compassion by my dolor and, if necessary, to convince him by means of threats: "Madeleine belongs to me; return her to me; I wish it!" The wretch must have quit Paris. Where is he hiding? No clue. Even the spiritist review died with Monsieur de Planor. I can't discover anything, I shan't know anything. My God, have pity!

---

1 What Macbeth actually says, addressing a doctor in Act 5 Scene 3, is "Throw physic to the dogs; I'll none of it."

10 March. The physician isn't content with me. He finds me nervous, agitated; he enjoins me to leave Paris as soon as possible. "You need mountain air," he told me this morning. "Leave immediately for one of the winter stations of Lake Geneva: Montreux, for example." Yes, certainly doctor, and that's an inspiration from Heaven! I shall be *en route* for Montreux tomorrow. Isn't it to the canton of Vaud that William Allis accompanied Monsieur de Planor last year? They were going to found a church there. Who knows? Perhaps I'll learn something out there!

Montreux, no date. Lake Geneva, azure waters, mirror of the azure of the heavens, the Dent de Jaman colored by so much verdure, the Dent du Midi, glaciers scintillating like diamonds in the sunlight, the insensible splendor of things, O Nature—I am one of your sons, however, and I am suffering and weeping. Why, then, your cruel indifference, bad mother, and why your disdainful smile?

Montreux, no date. I must be on the track, or rather, I have my man.

Today, in Montreux, I stopped in front of a bookshop. My attention had been alerted by a curious display of spiritist publications: theurgical pamphlets and periodicals brightening the shop window with their gaudy covers. And there, very prominent, an issue of *Redemption.* I went in. The merchant was busy selling an old English lady a stupid novel launched by advertising, and at first he paid no attention to me.

In an indifferent fashion—oh, I believe I played my role well—I reached for the pamphlet, grasped it, and went to sit down in a corner. It was a copy of the spiritist revue, already old; it bore the date of January, and announced the end of the publication on its cover. Still impassive—the shopkeeper was beginning to follow me with his eyes—I started leafing through the stupid rhapsody. To begin with, a necrological article on the poor and gentle Monsieur de Planor—much too brief and lacking in warmth, that eulogy. Then an account of his funeral, then a long and emphatic discourse in which William Allis protested against the "persecution" falling upon the Frères-unis in France; and finally, the announcement of an imminent exodus of that wretched church of sectarians.

Suddenly, I shivered, and my heart was gripped by anguish. On the last page of the periodical, I had read, printed in a large font, the following item:

> *Call for voluntary expiators. A letter has reached us from Calcutta: "A redoubtable epidemic is presently decimating the populations of India; the mortality is frightful, and several of our Frères-unis have been attained by the scourge. The shameful fanaticism of Christian sectarian priests refuses our beloved any help and any consolation. Can there not be found, among our sisters in Europe, voluntary expiatory souls who, in order to hasten deliverance, do not fear martyrdom? Our dying implore and God commands."*

The revue fell from my hands. I had understood. As a "voluntary expiator," Madeleine had responded to that appeal. She was confronting death at this moment, perhaps already dead. And it was Allis, the wretched William Allis, who had ordered all that!

In the meantime, the bookseller had approached me and was offering me his merchandise. I succeeded, not without difficulty, in repressing my emotion, and, still affecting indifference, said: "You are the depository of these spiritist publications?"

"Yes, of all our books of spiritualism," he said, using the more orthodox term.

Momentarily, I hesitated to lie, but, eventually arming myself with courage: "I'm a French Frère-uni myself."

"Ah!" he said. "Be welcome." He held out his hand to me.

"Is William Allis in Montreux?" I went on.

"Yes, but not for long. Here again, we're persecuted. All the evangelical pastors are declaiming and agitating 'the abomination of desolation.' The cantonal authorities might proscribe our worship."

"Where is the prophet staying?"

"Not far from here, in the Val des Avans, an hour's walk at the most."

"Unfortunately, I don't know the country very well."

The bookseller spread out a map of the environs of Montreux. "You see this road? Take it, and then go up this stream, which flows into the lake. It will take you into the Gorges de Chauderon, a picturesque agrarian region well known to tourists. When you reach the Gilon crossroads, you'll perceive a chalet on the right. Knock without fear, the prophet will open the door to you.

I took the map and paid him. "Thank you! Now I'll hasten to Allis."

The merchant approached me, and with a solemn gesture, placed his hand on my shoulder; his eyes were shining and his face had an expression of illuminate fanaticism. He lowered his voice.

"No, don't go to Allis today . . . tomorrow! At the moment he's in Lausanne, and won't be back until this evening. Oh, Monsieur, grave events are in preparation. Allis is bringing his friend Aleph among us—you must know Aleph, the most powerful medium of all, who not only incarnates but also materializes. The prophet has convened all our persecutors for the afternoon. A séance of psychomancy in the heart of Kursaal! The pastors and the atheists will come, and then . . . those who have eyes to see will see!"

Having spoken, my fanatic loosened his grip and addressed a fraternal salute to me. I left.

A few paces from the bookshop a perceived the shop of an armorer; there were several revolvers in the window display. I went in.

. . . .

. . . It was a house of banal aspect, one of those vulgar bourgeois chalets, the pretentious ugliness of which puts a stain on the austere and simple beauty of the Val des Avans. It stood on the summit of a mound, on the first undulations of the foothills of the mountain, all black in the blue-tinted whiteness poured out by the moon. The sky was limpid and luminous, scintillating with stars, with milky light spilling over the verdure of plants still pearled by the last winter snow. Beneath my feet, the distant and muffled murmur of La Baye de Montreux and the noise of waterfalls—but up above, in the immobile blackness of sinister fir-woods, there were all the terrors of the great silence.

I looked at my watch: nine o'clock. I made sure that my revolver was secure in my pocket and I began to climb the escarpment.

Suddenly, I stopped, shaken by a frisson. Very slow and soft, the sounds of an organ seemed to be reaching me; the plaint of a harmonium was emerging from the solitary house . . . and I recognize the same suppliant and funereal canticle once heard on the night and at the hour when Monsieur de Planor had died.

> *Day is breaking, come to me;*
> *Without you I cannot live . . .*

For whom were they weeping up there?

Hastening my steps, I continued my ascent.

Now I held myself against the house, on the lookout, listening. The door was closed; there was no light. In spite of the cold, however, a ground-floor window was open, as if to allow pale radiance of the moonlight to penetrate more easily . . . and the organ continued the modulations of the funerary melody.

Night is falling, come to me;
Without you I dare not die!

A few minutes went by, very long.

Finally, shaving the wall, I approached the window with furtive steps, and gently, slowly, I raised my head in order to look. Immediately, the music ceased and the door of the house was violently thrown open. A man appeared on the threshold and a voice—the voice of Allis—shouted at me: "Who dares to spy on our mysteries thus?"

I marched straight toward him.

"It's me, Allis, me . . . René Jaucourt."

"You?" he said, mildly. "What do you want, my poor Monsieur?"

A laugh of hateful anger prevented me from speaking at first, but: "I want Madeleine!"

The prophet looked at my face, red with fury, and then said, in his unctuous and tender voice: "Are you suffering a great deal, then, Monsieur? Well, come in . . . here, all is consolation."

Allis had closed the door on us, and, taking me by the hand, he guided me through the darkness. I soon found myself in the chamber with the open window, through which a few rays of moonlight were falling. The raw, wan clarity spread out over the parquet, and then, climbing the wall, caused the keys of a harmonium to gleam; but to the right and left of that luminous trail, the room remained absolutely obscure.

At first, my attention was attracted by something that was surely strange. In one of the dark corners of the room I thought I glimpsed a man lying full length on the floor. At times, he seemed to be motionless, an inert mass resembling a cadaver; at other times, a convulsion agitated him, he rose above the ground, and fell back immediately. At the same time, a dolorous, halting respiration escaped the body, punctuated by groans and plaintive sobs. A cyanophanic vapor, a kind of phosphorescent glow, exuded from that human form and floated above it. What was it?

"That," said William Allis, as if he had heard my thought, "is the medium Aleph. He has just entered into a trance; the soul that I was evoking just now is not far away."

The insolent serenity of the man exasperated me. Oho, charlatan, we're going to laugh? And I planted myself in front of him. "Are you going to return Madeleine to me?"

He folded his arms tranquilly, and smiled at me sadly.

"Henceforth, the penitent will perhaps be yours; she has submitted to her expiation."

"Enough grand words. Where is Madeleine?"

"Here! Call, and she will come; open your eyes, and you will recognize her."

The medium's groans augmented. Allis took a few steps in order to approach him . . . as for me, an anguishing stupor nailed me to the spot. Those words with a double meaning, those fateful words of the prophet were buzzing in my ears; I didn't understand, and yet I was frightened . . .

Suddenly, I uttered a clamor of despair: I had understood!

"Then . . . she's dead!"

Allis shook his head. "Nothing dies, and everything is life."

I responded with a howl of range. "Ah! You've killed her, bandit! Well, you're going to die too!"

But suddenly—oh, how, how did it happen?—an invisible force twisted my wrist; the weapon escaped my fingers, and I fell to my knees. The obscure sides of the room were suddenly illuminated; the floating vapor had taken on a form . . . the form of a woman . . . and before me—yes, yes, before me—stood Madeline, smiling and holding out her arms to me.

"Beloved, oh beloved . . . you!"

Recklessly, I launched myself toward her—and over my eyes, bathed with tears, I felt the caress of her hands pass over me; on my forehead and on my lips, I received the softness of her kiss . . . . . .

. . . .

✳

Paris (no date). At present, she is incessantly by my side . . . we belong to one another, and forever! By day she stands by the table where I am working, talking to me—silently—and advising me; I feel the subtle friction of her hair pass over my face, the ineffable freshness of her breath; by night, she appears to me again, smiling at all my dreams. Oh, my courage in the battle, my refuge in the dolor, my companion, my saint, my beloved!

Be blessed, then, Allis! Human amours are perishable; you have enabled me to acquire eternal amour!

. . . .

✳

Paris (no date). The physician has left my room, worried and shaking his head. He talked to my nurse in a whisper. I heard him . . .

Oh, beloved, finally!

Night is falling, come to me;
Without you I dare not die!

A PARTIAL LIST OF SNUGGLY BOOKS

G. ALBERT AURIER *Elsewhere and Other Stories*
S. HENRY BERTHOUD *Misanthropic Tales*
LÉON BLOY *The Tarantulas' Parlor and Other Unkind Tales*
ÉLÉMIR BOURGES *The Twilight of the Gods*
JAMES CHAMPAGNE *Harlem Smoke*
FÉLICIEN CHAMPSAUR *The Latin Orgy*
FÉLICIEN CHAMPSAUR *The Emerald Princess and Other Decadent Fantasies*
BRENDAN CONNELL *Clark*
BRENDAN CONNELL *Unofficial History of Pi Wei*
RAFAELA CONTRERAS *The Turquoise Ring and Other Stories*
ADOLFO COUVE *When I Think of My Missing Head*
QUENTIN S. CRISP *Aiaigasa*
QUENTIN S. CRISP *Graves*
QUENTIN S. CRISP *Rule Dementia!*
LADY DILKE *The Outcast Spirit and Other Stories*
CATHERINE DOUSTEYSSIER-KHOZE *The Beauty of the Death Cap*
BERIT ELLINGSEN *Now We Can See the Moon*
BERIT ELLINGSEN *Vessel and Solsvart*
ENRIQUE GÓMEZ CARRILLO *Sentimental Stories*
EDMOND AND JULES DE GONCOURT *Manette Salomon*
REMY DE GOURMONT *From a Faraway Land*
GUIDO GOZZANO *Alcina and Other Stories*
RHYS HUGHES *Cloud Farming in Wales*
J.-K. HUYSMANS *Knapsacks*
COLIN INSOLE *Valerie and Other Stories*
JUSTIN ISIS *Pleasant Tales II*
JUSTIN ISIS AND DANIEL CORRICK (editors)
    Drowning in Beauty: The Neo-Decadent Anthology
VICTOR JOLY *The Unknown Collaborator and Other Legendary Tales*
BERNARD LAZARE *The Mirror of Legends*
BERNARD LAZARE *The Torch-Bearers*
MAURICE LEVEL *The Shadow*
JEAN LORRAIN *Errant Vice*
JEAN LORRAIN *Masks in the Tapestry*
JEAN LORRAIN *Nightmares of an Ether-Drinker*
JEAN LORRAIN *The Soul-Drinker and Other Decadent Fantasies*

ARTHUR MACHEN *N*

ARTHUR MACHEN *Ornaments in Jade*

CAMILLE MAUCLAIR *The Frail Soul and Other Stories*

CATULLE MENDÈS *Bluebirds*

CATULLE MENDÈS *For Reading in the Bath*

ÉPHRAÏM MIKHAËL *Halyartes and Other Poems in Prose*

LUIS DE MIRANDA *Who Killed the Poet?*

OCTAVE MIRBEAU *The Death of Balzac*

TERESA WILMS MONTT *In the Stillness of Marble*

CHARLES MORICE *Babels, Balloons and Innocent Eyes*

DAMIAN MURPHY *Daughters of Apostasy*

DAMIAN MURPHY *The Star of Gnosia*

KRISTINE ONG MUSLIM *Butterfly Dream*

PHILOTHÉE O'NEDDY *The Enchanted Ring*

YARROW PAISLEY *Mendicant City*

URSULA PFLUG *Down From*

ADOLPHE RETTÉ *Misty Thule*

JEAN RICHEPIN *The Bull-Man and the Grasshopper*

DAVID RIX *A Suite in Four Windows*

FREDERICK ROLFE (Baron Corvo) *Amico di Sandro*

FREDERICK ROLFE (Baron Corvo)
  An Ossuary of the North Lagoon and Other Stories

JASON ROLFE *An Archive of Human Nonsense*

BRIAN STABLEFORD (editor)
  Decadence and Symbolism: A Showcase Anthology

BRIAN STABLEFORD *The Insubstantial Pageant*

BRIAN STABLEFORD *Spirits of the Vasty Deep*

COUNT ERIC STENBOCK *Studies of Death*

COUNT ERIC STENBOCK *Myrtle, Rue and Cypress*

MONTAGUE SUMMERS *Six Ghost Stories*

DOUGLAS THOMPSON *The Fallen West*

TOADHOUSE *Gone Fishing with Samy Rosenstock*

JANE DE LA VAUDÈRE *The Demi-Sexes and The Androgynes*

JANE DE LA VAUDÈRE *The Double Star and Other Occult Fantasies*

AUGUSTE VILLIERS DE L'ISLE-ADAM *Isis*

RENÉE VIVIEN *Lilith's Legacy*

RENÉE VIVIEN *A Woman Appeared to Me*

KAREL VAN DE WOESTIJNE *The Dying Peasant*

www.ingramcontent.com/pod-product-compliance
Lightning Source LLC
Chambersburg PA
CBHW050147110726

47898CB00008B/2699